BORN TO BE A DRAGON

By Eisley Jacobs

"Do not meddle in the affairs of dragons,
for you are crunchy and taste good with ketchup."
- Anonymous Dragon

DRAGONS FOREVER – BORN TO BE A DRAGON
http://DragonsForever.EisleyJacobs.com
All Rights Reserved
Original Copyright © 2011 by Eisley Jacobs
ISBN-13: 978-1456360962
ISBN-10: 1456360965

Cover art by Big House, Little Room Designs http://bighouselittleroom.EisleyJacobs.com

Edited by Debbie Lee http://www.writeawaydeb.com/

*This book is dedicated to my biggest fans,
my children. May you never stop
believing in the impossible.*

Chapter One
DEGLAN - THE DRAGON

Lightning jumped over the horizon and a tingle raced to the tip of my tail. The scales on my back vibrated as the power surged through me, working its way to my shoulders. The feeling settled on my right forearm.

The mark had changed... again.

I didn't want to look, but the intense desire built in my chest like the need for air. I gasped when my eyes rested upon the unmistakable black shape of a dragon burned into the flesh of my arm, with a ruby speck for the eye and spikes protruding down its spine.

Every dragon knew the legend. Hatchlings often played legend games, wishing they were the mighty dragon from the stories.

I swung the rock in my paw, skipping it over the waves rolling into the white sandy shore. Clouds bubbled like boiling water over the horizon to the west, where a storm brewed, pushing its way through the seas, forcing its wrath to Teken Island.

My best friend Carik joined me on the banks of the shore. He lifted his gray arm, trying to mimic my throw, but forgot to let go and ended up tossing his rock into the trees behind us.

"What do you think it means?" He'd watched me staring at the mark on my arm. He was the one dragon who knew it was morphing.

"I don't know, Carik. What if I'm *that* dragon?"

The words pinged in my head like the rock I'd skipped across the water. Rumors surfaced that Lord Edric was looking for the dragon from the legend. During each ten-year Rising Ceremony he checks marks and banishes the ones he thinks fit the legend's description. My tenth year celebration was coming, which meant I couldn't hide my mark any longer. He would find it under the lunar eclipse.

Then what? Would he banish my family and me? Or worse?

I couldn't let that happen.

"What are the chances, Deglan?" Carik chucked another rock. It went forward and sunk like a dead weight between the foamy waves.

"I know the chances are small, but what if? I can't just walk into the ceremony unprepared," I said, skipping another rock with ease.

Carik gave his head a frustrated shake. "Well yeah, but I still think you're overreacting. When's the last time it changed?"

I looked at my arm and groaned. "Two minutes ago."

"Are you serious?" He pulled my arm toward him. "Whoa. That's freaky."

I wrenched away from his grip.

"Thanks. That's just what I needed to hear."

"Do you really think it means…?"

"I don't know what it means, but it can't be good." I picked up another rock and inspected its smooth sides, then handed it to Carik. I positioned the first digit of his claw around the rock, followed by another, and showed him the motion again. Carik mimicked me, and the rock skipped across the waves easily.

"Yes!" He picked up another rock and flicked his arm. The rock plopped into the water a foot out, as if he'd just lobbed it in.

"It's all about digit placement," I said, and showed him again. "And don't drop your shoulder; keep it up and whisk the rock away across the waves."

Thunk.

The rock Carik threw hit the first wave and disappeared.

"I give up," he said, throwing his large gray body to the

beach. He looked like a hatchling throwing a tantrum with the way his limbs thrashed around in the sand. He released little grunts of anger each time he hit the ground.

"It just takes practice and determination." I skipped another rock across the tide, then sat beside my friend.

The sun dipped into the horizon, casting the last of its warmth over us.

Carik smacked the beach one last time, spraying a curtain of grains floating through the air. He sat up and pushed his large gray feet into the sand, his claws barely visible. "So, what are you going to do?"

"I don't know. I should probably tell my parents, especially if they'll be banished when Lord Edric finds out."

"I still don't see how you've kept it hidden from them all these years. You'd think they would have noticed by now."

I shrugged. "The couple times my mom has mentioned something, I played it off as a smudge of volcanic rock." I grabbed my tail and waved it at him. "It's not that far a stretch considering we're covered in it all the time."

Carik studied his own mark, shaped like a disjointed star. "Maybe your mark is part of another legend we don't know about. Maybe Lord Edric will see it and you will be a lord or something."

His hopeful tone made me smile. "Yeah, maybe you're right," I said, but the churning in my stomach made me believe it only meant trouble. The rumble of thunder overhead seemed to confirm it.

"We should get back," I said, watching the clouds roll at an alarming speed toward the island.

I tried to keep my tone light as we walked, but found it difficult when each step was harder than the last. When my dwelling came into view, I couldn't help but groan.

Carik grabbed my arm, which made me freeze. He bolted forward, through my dwelling gate, and snatched up the garden gnome who'd just been collecting mushrooms.

"Ha! I got you!"

I ran to the gnome's aid. "Carik, leave him alone! Didn't

he already call truce?"

Carik laughed. "There's no such thing as truce to a dragon."

Philip, the garden gnome he tormented *this* time, winked at me then dropped his sack on Carik's foot. Carik screeched then opened his claw in surprise. Philip jumped to the ground and dove for his burrow, narrowly missing Carik's swipe.

"If you aren't careful," I said, pointing at the other side of the lawn, "the whole lot of 'em will revolt when your back's turned. I've seen it and it isn't pretty."

Carik laughed again as Philip peeked his head from the earth. When Carik growled, Philip darted back inside.

"So, you *are* going to tell them tonight, right?"

I rubbed the back of my neck, willing the stress to disappear. "Yeah. I guess I have to."

"You know..." Carik began, then rambled on about the mysteries of dragon marks, acting all philosophical, while I watched Philip's small red hat poke out of the burrow. He put his hand to his lips and crept out, slowly reaching for his mushroom bag. I looked at Carik, not listening to a word he said, then back to Philip. I gave him a quick nod, then he scurried for the bag.

"Ha!" Carik yelled mid-sentence and caught the poor gnome by the foot, dangling him upside down. "Thought you could outsmart me?"

"You're so asking for it." I watched Philip kick his free leg and flail at my friend. "When they decide to fight back, I'm going to hold you down."

Carik narrowed his eyes. He shrugged, then dropped the gnome, who flipped midair and landed on his feet, just like a cat. Philip scrunched up his face in a sour expression when he grabbed for his sack. He then turned and wiggled his rear at Carik.

"Why that little..." Carik scrambled for the gnome, but missed him by an inch as he ducked into his burrow and disappeared. "How can you stand those guys?"

I shrugged. "They keep the yard free of pests." I looked sideways at Carik. "Huh? It's not working."

"Har har har." He turned toward the road. "See you tomorrow at instruction," he said, turning once to bump claws with me. Carik was a good dragon... even if he liked to torture the help.

Lightning flashed overhead, sending the same feeling rolling through my veins. I waited for the boom of thunder, knowing it wasn't far behind. But no sound came from the sky. Instead a frog nearby gave out a bellow of a croak.

I hesitated at the door of my dwelling, wondering how to begin the conversation with my parents.

"Nasty storm out there tonight." Dad stepped out from behind the shrubs nearby, just as the thunder cracked overhead.

I jumped back against the door. "Dad, don't do that," I said, clutching my chest.

Another flash of lightning streaked across the sky and the thunder clapped, sending pain through my body. I cringed and grabbed my arm. It felt like someone was pressing a hot iron to the scales.

"Deglan, what is it?" Dad said, grasping my shoulder.

I knew if I didn't speak now I would lose the nerve to say anything at all. I removed the claw from my arm and watched as his eyes drifted to the dragon mark.

"Deglan, what's that?" He pulled my arm closer to the light.

"It's my mark."

"This isn't the mark you were hatched with, son." His voice shook with panic.

"I know. It's... It's been changing," I whispered.

"For how long?" The veins in Dad's neck throbbed as he searched my face for answers.

"I don't know. One day the mark was crescent-shaped and the next it was distorted. I didn't think anything of it because it didn't look like..." I hesitated. "Then I just thought something was wrong with me. It didn't take shape until recently, when it began changing every day, morphing into what it is now."

Dad's eyes went blank as if he were lost in thought.

"I thought we received our marks the moment the light comes through our shells after we break it. It's not supposed to change unless..."

"Shhh," he said, cutting me off. "Does anyone know about this?"

I shook my head. "Why is it changing?" The quiver in my voice was difficult to mask.

"Deglan..." Dad put his claw on my shoulder, his star shape mark mocking the seriousness of it all. "Why don't we talk about this tomorrow when I've had some time to think... okay?"

My stomach clenched as I read the horror in my father's eyes. We would be banished for this. There was no way to hide it now. I would be a ten year at the next lunar eclipse and Lord Edric would see it and cast us away... or worse.

Chapter Two
MEIA - THE HUMAN

Ms. Keller pushed her large brown curls away from her face and tried to smile, but I could tell she wasn't exactly sure what she should say. We'd had this conversation at least once a week since I'd been enrolled in Turner Elementary four months ago.

Her eyebrows knit together, then softened. "Meia, I know it's hard for you to have a new set of expectations at home, but I don't think I'm asking too much for you to pay attention in class."

A long, labored sigh escaped my lips. "I don't try to daydream, it just... sorta... happens. One minute I'm listening to you babble on about the earth's core, the next minute I'm excavating to find the center of the earth."

She studied me, then crossed her arms over her body. "Can you try harder?"

"I'll try, Ms. Keller. I really will." I tried to sound like I really meant it. I needed to escape these four walls and disappear into the afternoon sun. She lifted her mouth into a lopsided grin, then dismissed me.

My best friend, Cate, swung in time with the others when I appeared next to the metal swing set that was in dire need of a new coat of paint. Her long black hair covered her face when she stopped to talk with me.

"What were you daydreaming about *this* time?" She said, pushing her hair from her eyes.

I sat in the empty rubber seat and pushed off, ready to soar high above the problems of the fourth grade. "Same stuff as always." I glanced sideways at Cate, trying to match her height. "I told Ms. Keller it was about her lesson, though. I thought it would be easier for her to accept."

"Yeah, if you go spouting you were daydreaming about dragons—"

I slammed my feet into the woodchips. They sprayed in every direction as I grabbed Cate's swing and spun her to face me. "Shhhhhh! Don't tell the whole world." I looked down the line of swings, relieved no one had heard.

Cate clasped her hands over her mouth and mumbled through her fingers, "Sorry."

I let go of her swing. "It's okay." I looked over at Patricia Tison, who skipped rope with the other girls near the tetherball court. She frowned when our eyes connected. I had no idea why Patricia didn't like me. I couldn't ask her why either, because I made it a point to stay as far away from her group as possible. She'd been the reason Ms. Keller called upon me, pointing out I was on the wrong page of our lesson. I glared at her and wished she would burst into flames, but I knew that probably wasn't appropriate.

"You wanna race?" I pushed back and stood, ready for a head-to-head with Cate.

"You're on!" She pushed her swing back.

The rubber mat rested just below my armpits and I gripped the chains as high as my arms could possibly reach. "Ready? One... Two... Three!"

We gathered our feet up and plopped into the seats, pushing off the ground as we rose. Pumping my feet hard, I gained height. Exhilaration rushed over me as the wind whipped my long brown hair back and forth. I climbed higher and higher. At the pinnacle, I looked over at Cate, who struggled as she tried to reach me.

"I win!"

We both giggled and continued to fly through the air on the rubber magic carpets. I leaned back with my eyes closed and imagined I was on the back of a dragon, soaring high above the playground and its cares.

After school, Cate and I walked down the street with the afternoon sun heavy on our backs. She eyed me, as if counting the hordes of freckles dotting my nose. I knew she wanted to ask about my dreams; she was always curious what the blue dragon was up to. It was like my own personal television series in my head.

"You know I don't like talking about it out in the open. People already think I'm weird. I don't need to give them more reason to believe it's true."

"I know, but it's so cool! Did you tell Mrs. Bensen this morning? What did she say?"

I laughed. My new foster parents were an exception to all other families I'd had over the years. The Bensens encouraged me to share my dreams. At first it was hard to share with them, thinking they would consider me crazy. But I had to admit, it had become much easier to share them, instead of hiding them away. It made them even more real, which was fine by me.

"No, I woke up late this morning."

"At least you finally have someone who understands," she said, stopping at the corner.

Her words stung. I'd overheard Mrs. Bensen on the phone with my social worker the previous week. It sounded like she was looking for a new placement, but I hadn't told Cate yet. We were lucky the last placement had put me back in her school district. We'd kept in touch when I moved homes, but it wasn't like attending the same school. Much rejoicing could be heard on the playground my first day back.

Cate and I parted at the corner, both groaning over the homework load in our backpacks. Ms. Keller might have been one of the nicest teachers in our school, but she still dished out a lot of homework almost every day.

I walked the remainder of the way to the Bensen's white cottage, thinking about the probability of a new foster home. There had to be a way to convince my brain that dragons weren't real and to move on to princesses or fairies or something normal for a girl. However, even as I thought about the possibility, I knew it wasn't what I actually wanted to do. I loved living in my dreams and even relished the nightmares. I always believed that if I kept them close, I would be safe, even if it meant I was a *marked* foster child. And marked I was. My issues were written all over my papers.

Mrs. Bensen sat at the table when I opened the white Victorian screen. "How was school?" she said, pushing back the red mass of curls draped over her face.

Oh no. I could tell by the way she tapped the mug between her fingers, she knew something. "Fine." I grabbed a cookie from the plate and made my way across the kitchen, hoping to escape the interrogation.

"Ms. Keller called."

I froze in my tracks. *Busted.*

Mrs. Bensen raised an eyebrow and waited to see if I would divulge any information. When I didn't, she continued. "She said you had a rough day."

I hung my head. "It wasn't *that* rough," I said, my mouth full of the warm, homemade chocolate chip cookie. When she didn't say anything else, I looked up and met her expectant eyes. Of all the foster parents I'd had, Mr. and Mrs. Bensen were the nicest and most understanding of the bunch, which made the conversation I'd overhead even harder to accept.

"Do you have homework?" she said, rising from the table with her pink Susan G. Komen coffee cup.

"When do I *not* have homework? I swear she's out to ruin the fourth grade."

"We don't swear in this house."

I groaned, wondering when I would remember their rules. "Oh. Sorry, I forgot." Maybe that was why she wanted a new placement.

"Just a reminder. Why don't you head upstairs and get started?"

"Oh joy." I grabbed for another cookie before I turned and ran up the stairs, skipping every other one.

"Goodness!" Mr. Bensen boomed from somewhere at the top of the stairs. "Did a herd of elephants get through the front door again?" He appeared from his office, glasses perched on his nose, his brown hair cut to perfection. "Oh! It's not elephants, its Meia." He greeted me with his customary wide smile and wink.

"Sorry," I apologized, tiptoeing across the landing toward my room.

"It's okay, kiddo; I was coming out to say hello. How was school?"

"Did Ms. Keller call you too?" My voice raised an octave when the words left my lips.

He laughed. "No, no. I don't know anything about a phone call." He raised one of his eyebrows, cocked his head to the side, and leaned closer. "You didn't burn down the school, did you?"

I couldn't hold back the laughter that erupted from my belly. "No, but I wished a girl would have burst into flames today." The shock on his face told me I'd said too much. "I didn't really wish her to burst into flames," I added, hoping to soothe the alarm. I couldn't bear to look him in the face. "She tattled on me during Earth Science." I tugged on my backpack, unsure of what to say. If I stood there long enough, I would seal the deal on my new placement. "I need to research an island for history," I said, trying to change the subject. "May I have some internet time?"

"Sure, Squirt. I'll unlock the kid controls for you."

"Thanks," I said, then dashed into my room.

"Meia?"

I peeked my head from the room and saw my foster father's warm smile.

"Yeah?"

"What island do you need to research?"

"Oh, it can be any island. We are just learning about how they form." If I wasn't mistaken, Mr. Bensen had a mischievous gleam in his eyes, one I'd never witnessed. "Start in the Pacific Ocean; there are some cool islands over there, like the Cook Islands." He turned without another word, then headed back into his office.

Chapter Three
DEGLAN · THE DRAGON

In my room, I looked out over the yard, the steady hum of the crickets announced the approaching storm. Philip, the garden gnome, sat by the fishpond with a pole dipped into its waters. He looked up and waved, then snatched the line and pulled up one of Mom's goldfish. The gnome could barely contain his excitement as he danced throughout the yard, dangling the fish from his string. He grabbed the fish with both hands, kissed it square on the lips, then tossed it back into the pond. I shook my head and smiled.

Philip turned to wave, but froze with his hand halfway in gesture. He spun around and stared into the night sky, twitching his nose, sniffing the breeze. He faced me once more, his eyes boring holes into mine. His large bushy eyebrows shot together and he bade me a quick farewell and scampered away, leaving his pole by the pond.

A chill raced up my tail, over my scales, and rested at the base of my skull. Something was wrong. The clouds tumbled and seethed outside the window, as if their mission was to encompass the world in darkness. It grew dark so quickly, I couldn't even see the fishing pole the gnome had left. The only light came from a small torch on the wall in my room.

I ran my fingers over the mark on my arm and marveled at the change, the tingle still evident as the face of the dragon peered up at me.

Could it really mean...?

I shook my head, rubbed my face, and lay upon my pallet. Dad promised we would talk tomorrow. However, something deep in the pit of my stomach told me tomorrow might be too late.

I'd only been asleep a few hours before something startled me awake. The glowing embers from the torch on the wall cast a ghostly red haze around the room. I sat up, wondering what had awoken me. I shot to my feet when I felt a poke on my leg.

Carik knelt nearby, his arm resting on my bed just under the window, his eyes wide.

"What are you doing here?" I couldn't help the annoyed tone that escaped. He'd woken me up in the early morning hours before for a scavenger hunt. But this was a very bad time.

His voice was barely audible over the gale force wind outside my window. "They're coming, Deglan."

I frowned, wondering what type of game we were going to play tonight. Rubbing my cheek, I looked towards the window, then froze. A few dwellings away, a dragon held a torch above his head. When he lowered it, the blood froze in my veins. There were at least twenty-five adult dragons gathered in the street. I ducked from the window when one turned his head in my direction. "Carik, what is going on?"

Carik peeked out the window and ducked again. "It wasn't me!" He spat, guilt written all over his pale gray face. He looked like he was going to pass out.

"What did you do Carik? Who did you tell?"

He rubbed his eyes and let out a big sigh. "I maybe mentioned it to one person, but he was sworn to secrecy!"

A low growl vibrated in the back of my throat and I pulled Carik to his feet. "Who did you tell Carik?"

"It doesn't matter Deglan, you have to go. This is serious stuff. I heard..." he paused, pulling himself from my grasp. "You just need to go."

My heart stammered in my chest when I looked out the window at the restless crowd. "I have to warn my parents," I said and dashed for the door.

I raced to the main dwelling area, Carik following closely behind. To my surprise, my parents were up and working frantically on a knapsack. Mom tossed in dried meats, while Dad shoved fruit into its bulging sides.

"Mom? Dad?" The words came out like a frightened hatchling after a bad dream.

"Deglan!" My mom rushed to my side, hugged me, then turned my arm over to look at my mark.

Dad tied off the bag and put it into a leather backpack. "We don't have time to explain. You have to flee."

"What? Why? I don't understand."

An elder-gnome burst through the back door. "They're moving," he said, urgency tight in his voice. He looked between my parents.

"Stall them!" Dad commanded. The gnome nodded, then vanished. Dad shoved a book into the pack, then snapped it shut. "Deglan, you have to leave this place."

At his words, waves of terror flooded over me. "Where do I go?"

Dad helped me with the leather backpack and took hold of my shoulders. "Let your dreams guide you." He glanced at Carik then back to me.

"What?" I heard the disbelief in my voice. What did he mean?

"Deglan," Mom said, emotion thick in her words. "Listen to your father. We don't have time to explain. Just go." Her voice broke. "Please," she pleaded.

I darted forward and took hold of my mom. My dad joined us in the embrace, then pried me from her grasp.

"Deglan. Go," he said, passing me off to Carik like they'd planned this getaway. "Your mother and I will be fine. Go."

Carik pulled me through the door, into the darkness. Pounding footsteps echoed around us... or was it the sound of my heart. I couldn't be sure.

We raced through the dark forest behind my dwelling, blending into the backdrop of the night. At the top of the hill, I pulled away from Carik and looked back at my dwelling. The dragons were in my yard struggling with the gnomes. Though they were small, the gnomes did a good job creating the diversion. One broke away from the pack and rushed for the door.

"Deglan, we have to find a place to hide."

We stumbled through the dense underbrush toward the beach, the angry storm covering the moon, making it nearly impossible to remain upright. We scaled the nearest cliff side as fast as our limbs would allow.

"Should we try and fly?" I asked between pants.

"We can't fly Deglan, we haven't been through the Rising yet," he said pulling himself up the cliff.

He was right. We hadn't been through our tenth year Rising Ceremony yet. Under the lunar eclipse, young dragons earned their rights to fly. No one knew if the light of the eclipse allows us to fly or if it was something to do with the blessing the lord bestows upon us. Now we may never know.

We crawled across the rocks like a salamander looking for food, hoping for an opening — anything large enough to hide ourselves in. We needed to get out of sight, at least until we decided on a plan.

My claw grasped the top of an opening and I pulled myself up to peer inside. "Carik, in here!" I called.

We pressed ourselves inside, barely enough room to move.

"Deglan, what are you going to do?"

I leaned my head against the rocks behind me. "I don't know, Carik. Dad said to follow my dreams, but I don't know what that means." I closed my eyes, fatigue settling over my body in the small space. "What are you going to do Carik? Why did you come with me?"

He was silent for a long moment before he allowed a deep sign to escape. "I'm sorry, Deglan."

"Why are you sorry Carik?" Even as I said it, I knew why.

"I told Blake. You'd think brothers would keep secrets, but I guess he been told if he'd ever heard anything... I had no idea he'd rat on you."

"It's okay Carik," I said, patting his leg. "You didn't know. Besides, it was bound to come out."

"So then, it really does mean..."

"Maybe."

We sat in silence, listening for noises on the beach. My body trembled and my eyes fought to stay open. If we stayed here, it would only be a matter of time before they found us. My mind struggled with what to do as the exhaustion overtook me.

I didn't remember falling asleep, but when I saw the small speckle-faced human standing on top of the cliffs, I knew I was dreaming. She watched me with unwavering eyes, willing me to understand as she pointed over the water toward the unknown. She had no emotion on her face, yet her eyes danced as she stared at me. She wanted me to follow her.

A beacon of light parted the clouds and illuminated the place she stood, casting a warm glow over the girl. I took a step toward her then she vanished when a light flashed overhead. The ground shook under my feet, which had nothing to do with the waves below. A pack of dragons appeared from the cliff side, their faces pressed hard with anger. Soon dragons stalked me from every direction but the air.

Panic flooded my veins as they inched closer. I knew they were intent on something more than an evening stroll. The one closest to me held something small in his arms as he lumbered forward. When he stopped, I realized it was the girl. Her brown hair flowed over her brow and hung limp like the rest of her body. She looked so small and fragile in the arms of the massive beast that held her. I looked among the angry faces and realized they were there to kill both the girl... and me.

"You are forbidden to associate with humans," Lord Edric's voice echoed over the cliff.

I couldn't see him, but I knew he was there. Without another word, the dragon holding the human girl let her go, intending to drop her to the hard ground. The girl was in my arms before a second had passed. The moment her pale, soft skin touched mine, a jolt of energy shot through my veins and I heard her thoughts.

You must flee.

The murmur grew louder and their faces rigid with a mixture of fear and awe as I growled protectively. With unmatched speed, I darted toward the edge of the cliff, clutching the girl in my arms. I didn't stop at the edge but jumped from the cliff side chased by the roars of disapproval. I spread my full-grown wings over the water and was out of sight in seconds. I flew southwest, guided by the thoughts of the unconscious girl in my arms.

A clap of thunder startled me from the dream. My father's words waved over me like the mist. *Let your dreams guide you.* Sweat poured off my scales and the dream rattled through my head, the face of the girl burning itself into my memory.

"Carik?" I gasped. "I've got to go."

Chapter Four
MEIA - THE HUMAN

I didn't know why Mr. Bensen wanted me to start with the Cook Islands, but I was glad he'd suggested it when pictures of the breathtaking islands, called atolls, popped onto my screen. I discovered atolls were volcanoes that had collapsed over time and were now islands of coral with a lagoon in the middle. Sometimes the lagoon is completely closed off from the ocean and other times only partially. They almost looked like a grand rendition of my oatmeal bowl some mornings after Mrs. Bensen added the milk.

Picture after picture of the beautiful islands and their peoples filled my screen and made it nearly impossible for me to choose one for my assignment. Near the bottom of the alphabetical list of the Cook Islands, the Penrhyn atoll caught my eye with its strange amoeba-like shape and large lagoon in the middle. The waters were bluer than any I'd seen. It was hard to believe this color was part of the Pacific Ocean. The white sands of Penrhyn sparkled, creating a sense of peace as I scrolled through the photos. According to the article, the Cook Island atolls were the most unspoiled atolls on Earth.

I filled out Ms. Keller's questionnaire using the Penrhyn as my choice, indicating the island group and its coordinates. The last part of the assignment was to write a short paragraph on what we might find if we went to the island we'd chosen. Tapping my pencil on my chin, I knew I could come up with a fantastic story that included dragons. With a cool-shaped island like that, anything was possible. I groaned when I realized it wouldn't thrill Ms. Keller to read about my daydreams. I'd tried that once and received an A for effort but a D as my grade, which was as close to an F as I'd ever been.

I scanned through the images again, looking for wildlife, and found the albatross and the blue heron. I clicked from the images to Google, and read the first link.

"*My Journey Through the Cook Island Atolls*," I read aloud, then clicked the link.

An old man with a friendly, but scruffy, face stared at me from the corner of the webpage. His name was Atticus. The rest of the page looked like notes from his journey, complete with dates, times, and a few snapshots. I knew my computer time was nearly over, but I really wanted to be able to read what this man had written.

"Mr. Bensen?" I said, standing at the door of his office again.

"Yes, Meia?" he said, his head bent over his work.

"May I print a webpage on the Cook Island atolls?"

He looked up and smiled. I could tell he was happy I'd taken his suggestion. "Of course, Meia. I'll make sure the printer is loaded with paper."

I skipped back to my room and pressed print. I dashed back into the office as the inkjet roared to life and spit the pages out one-by-one into my waiting grasp.

"Got what you need?" Mr. Bensen said over my shoulder when I stapled them.

"Yeah, thanks."

Back in my room, I set the printout on the desk and scribbled a paragraph on the albatross. Luckily, I'd done some research on this powerful bird last year, so the knowledge was easy to recall. I eyed the stapled papers beside me but knew I needed to complete the other assignments before dinner. I may be a little unbalanced in many ways, but I knew my grades were important. The other two assignments were easy, even the math one, which was a relief. Fractions were not my idea of a good time.

I grabbed Atticus' article and darted down the stairs,

headed to the back porch hammock. My feet slid to a halt in the kitchen, where Mrs. Bensen stood cutting veggies.

"Do you need anything from me?" I reached for another cookie.

"Did you get your homework done?" She turned and spied the papers in my hand.

"Yep, I had to do a questionnaire and paragraph on islands. Mr. Bensen suggested I do it on a Cook island. Have you ever seen the Cook Islands?"

She laughed. "It makes sense he told you to look there. We were married on Rarotonga, one of the southernmost islands."

"Really? So you got to see all the cool lagoons and stuff?"

"Yes, we were able to visit all the Cook Islands while we were there. It was lovely. You'd like it there," she said.

My mind wandered into the atolls and lagoons inside them. I could almost smell the warm, salty water in the air.

"Have fun reading. I'll call you for dinner in a few."

The time-worn hammock swayed lightly under my weight as I situated myself in its blanket of webs. The sides curled up around me like a cocoon, wrapping me in safety. Floating off the ground and feeling the wind on all sides of me, allowed me to think and dream with no regards to the world.

Mrs. Bensen smiled at me through the window. I knew I was lucky to have this foster placement and hoped there was no truth to what I'd overheard. The Bensens were empty nesters and only certified for one child, which was fine by me. Most of my past problems had to do with other children in the household not liking me or the parents freaking out that I might influence them to be as weird as I was. I didn't think I was weird, just imaginative.

The papers in my hand rustled with the slight evening breeze and begged for my attention. The soft light filtered over the papers as I began to read, recreating the journey in my mind.

Atticus chronicled every bit of his adventure through all fifteen Cook Island atolls. He noted anything and everything about each atoll that he could — temperature of the day, how long he stayed, what he saw, and people he encountered. The pictures stuffed throughout the article were as beautiful as the ones I'd already seen, but from ground level, they looked more real and inviting.

I walked with Atticus as he visited the streets of Rarotonga. When he wrote about a wedding, I wondered if it had been the Bensen's, but knew that was highly unlikely. I felt the wind in my hair as he wrote about the trip between the southern islands, and even got seasick when he spoke of the longer trek through the murky, turbulent waters between Palmerston and Suwarrow. I heard the birds cry when he traveled by foot through Nassau island, the only one of the northern group without a lagoon. When he spoke about Rakahanga, I could feel the warm sand beneath my bare feet and the sun shining heavy on my head as it had for him. I imagined the fish dancing on the reef and the sea turtle that swam past him as he snorkeled in the lagoon.

I sensed his disappointment when he boated two hundred miles and arrived at the final Cook Island, the one from my assignment — Penrhyn, the largest atoll in all the Pacific Ocean. He wasn't disappointed because of the atoll; He was disappointed the adventure had ended… and I was too.

My heart wiggled in my chest when Atticus explored the large lagoon and the outer reefs of Penrhyn. The sharks swam right up to his boat, nudging the sides with their long, slender bodies.

I wasn't ready for the adventure to end. I wanted to reread the whole thing again and live the journey once more. The whole time I read I felt as though I had been flying with him, unseen in his travels, and I was anxious to do it again.

The text ended in the middle of the page with a *Back to the Top* link printed on the bottom, which was strange because another page stuck out oddly from beneath my fingers. I flipped to the last page and grinned. Atticus had indeed written about all the Cook Islands, but the last page recorded the accidental discovery of an additional island not on any map.

Atticus' navigation systems had failed and he found himself northeast of the Cook Islands. When his system glitch resolved, he found himself at 138 degrees east and 15 degrees north. After getting back on course, he headed for the nearest island on his map, still a few hundred miles away. However, just a few miles out, an island rose like a beacon in the distance. Checking the coordinates against his map, he knew no island should exist there.

Under a nearly full lunar eclipse, he neared the island to make anchor. A loud clamoring of roars ruptured the air, causing Atticus to pull up his anchor and speed away from the island. He watched through the cover of the red eclipsed moon as massive beasts rose from the trees and headed straight toward him. He shoved his second motor down and put both on high, carrying him to safety.

My heart leapt into my throat when I read his next line.

"If I hadn't known I was hallucinating from the long day's travels, I would have sworn the beasts that rose over the unknown island were dragons."

Dragons.

Chapter Five
DEGLAN - THE DRAGON

A loud clash on the beach below told me we weren't alone. I didn't know what to do, or where to go, but I knew I needed to get off the island.

"Up there!" A voice echoed.

My heart dropped into my stomach like an anchor pushed off the port bow.

"Carik, what do we do?" My words came out as a plea.

Carik grabbed my shoulders and brought his face close to mine. "I got you in this mess, Deglan, I'm going to get you out."

He darted for the opening before I could grab him.

"What are you going to do?"

"I'm going to buy you some time. It's dark enough, they won't know what dragon they're chasing."

"What happens if they catch you?"

The moonlight flickered on Carik's face and I could see the wary smile. "I'll make something up. I'm good at that." He tried to give me an encouraging smile but I could tell he was as frightened as I was. "Just get away, Deglan. I know for a fact they don't just want to talk."

I gulped hard and watched my friend leave. I waited for the voices to grow distant then scrambled from my hiding place, making my way up the cliff, intent on following the command from my dreams. At the top, I raced to the edge closest to the ocean, wondering if the dream meant I could fly. The darkness obscured my view of the ocean below. I couldn't remember how far I'd climbed, but I knew if my wings didn't work, I'd not live through the fall.

The echo of wings brought my attention back to the cliff. I whipped my head in every direction and gasped when a small break in the storm clouds silhouetted the coming dragons. The first dragon landed with a thump, followed by several more. They stood in silent ranks, their eyes boring holes in my courage.

My mind searched for a way out, but when another set of dragons touched down, I knew there was no hope of escaping this rage. I backed toward the cliff's edge, hoping Carik was safe, racing for home and not captured.

I clenched my jaw, trying to hold off the tremors shaking my limbs. If they captured me, what would happen to my parents? It was at that moment the idea came, like a bolt of lightning hitting its target. I glanced at the turbulent waters below. If I could make it look like I had plunged to my death, maybe they would leave my family alone. I could dash from the cliff face masked in the darkness of the storm. Once out of sight, I could use a dragon's basic instinct and fly. Surely, there was nothing more to it. I knew the plan was crazy, but I didn't see another option.

Three more dragons circled the cliff face, their powerful wings raking the air with thunderous strokes. Lord Edric was in the center.

Panic rose in my chest, threatening to cut the airflow to my lungs. I didn't know if I could go through with my plan. I turned toward the ocean and drew in a long, deep breath.

"Deglan," said Lord Edric in a soothing voice. If I hadn't known he was out to get me, I would have listened to anything he said. "There's no reason to be afraid, Deglan."

The ground shuddered under his mighty steps as he slowly came closer.

My heart trembled in my chest. The clouds rolled over the moon, stabbing the cliff in darkness again. I turned, unable to see Lord Edric as he stalked forward.

"I'm going to make this easy for you," I said, trying to sound brave. "Tell my parents I love them."

"What are you going to do, Deglan? You can't fly yet."

I hoped he was wrong; my whole plan hinged upon just how wrong he was.

"Let me see your mark, Deglan," Lord Edric said, now dangerously close.

I turned and looked down into the black void below. I couldn't see the waves, which meant they couldn't either.

"Just tell them... please."

The last bit came out in a croak, and I threw myself over the edge. The wind rushed between my horns as I plummeted toward the ocean. I fought the urge to open my wings, knowing they watched from the top.

I searched for the ocean below, my heart still throbbing in uncontrollable beats.

The fear concentrated in my veins, icy and intense, pulling me toward the unknown. The white, angry, foaming waves appeared, and in the same instant, I thrust my wings out and prayed for instinct to kick in.

The wind caught the membranes between my bones, and my stomach fell into my feet. The weightlessness hit me as I soared over the roaring tide. I tucked my arms and legs under my body, as I had seen others do. I whipped my tail, catching it on the streams of air that pushed in every direction.

It worked! I was flying.

Chapter Six
MEIA - THE HUMAN

At the dinner table, everyone was silent as we listened to the Cubs baseball game on the WGN Radio Network. The only sounds from us were the groans when someone didn't get on base or when someone else did. Usually, I listened intently to the game, but tonight my mind pinged with questions about Atticus and the possible dragons. I knew I shouldn't bring them up at dinner, but I wondered if Atticus had written other chronicles of his journeys or even if he'd gone back to explore the hidden island.

With the dishes washed and the "Go Cubs Go" song playing in the background, I headed upstairs for my nightly routine. Maybe Mr. Bensen would allow me five more minutes on the computer. Atticus' website address was printed across the bottom of the page, so I knew I could find him again, maybe discover something, or even email him. When I asked for more time, Mr. Bensen didn't question it, which was good because I didn't want to lie to him. I may be a daydreamer, but I'm not a liar.

Once in front of the computer, I pulled up the address from my crinkled papers. The heading had links I hadn't visited before, and I clicked them all open into new windows. Atticus had been to many other island chains, but a quick search of the pages provided no mention of dragons. At the bottom of the page was a FAQ section, which I knew stood for Frequently Asked Questions. I read though the questions, disappointed again when none mentioned the Cook Islands or dragons.

My breath caught in my throat when I saw a link called "Contact Me." I clicked it quickly, knowing my time was almost up.

Dear Mr. Atticus, My name is Meia. I'm ten-years-old and found your webpage *My Journey Through the Cook Island Atolls* on the internet when doing a report for my fourth grade homework. I'm wondering if you went back to 138 degrees east and 15 degrees north. And if you did, what did you find? If you didn't, may I ask why? Thank you very much for emailing me back, Meia

I clicked "Send" and watched as the email loaded into the status bar and froze there. *Could my internet time have expired already?* I tapped my fingers on the desk, trying to be patient. When the status bar completed its voyage, I couldn't help but squeal with delight.

Having tucked me into bed, Mrs. Bensen turned out the light and shut my door. I had stuffed the papers under my pillow right before she came up. Their room was right below mine, and I found out really quick they could hear me walking on the floor. They allowed me to read at night, but I didn't want to explain why I'd chosen to read again about the Cook Island atolls.

I kissed the book light I'd received for Christmas four foster families ago and flipped it on. The light illuminated the small room, casting long shadows on the floor. I sat against my pillow, leaned on the back wall, and began to read the words of Atticus again. Like before and probably every time after, his words created a beautiful picture in my head. When I arrived at the last page, I read each paragraph four times before moving on, careful not to miss any hidden clues written between the lines. When I reached the last line, I read it over and over and over… and over again.

Dragons.

They were real; I knew it. I had always known it. Now, I had to talk to this Atticus guy and find out if he saw anything else. I held the papers against my chest and sighed. Maybe, just maybe, there would be some truth to my daydreams.

The computer on the desk made a soft *DING*, which I recognized immediately as my email. Mr. Bensen must have mistyped the time to cut off my internet access. I didn't get many emails, especially not ones this late at night. My friends were already in bed, so the email must be from Atticus. It had been at least an hour since Mrs. Bensen had put me to bed, so it wouldn't be out of the ordinary for me to get up and use the bathroom.

The floor was cool under my bare feet as I tiptoed toward the computer. I moved the mouse quickly and clicked the email icon. When it came up, I could have danced with delight, not caring who heard; it was indeed from Atticus. I opened the message, then hurried to the bathroom, careful to click the door shut with more force than needed, so they would realize where I was. My heart fluttered with expectation as I spent the appropriate time procrastinating before washing my hands and heading through the dark hall toward my room. I pushed the door shut again, then tiptoed to the computer and sat. My heart slammed against my chest as I read the words on the computer screen.

> Dear Meia,
> Isn't it past your bedtime? I'm curious why you want to know if I went back to the island. You are the first person to ask. Ever.
>   Sincerely, Atticus

I pressed "Reply" and typed out a single sentence:

> I want to know more about the beasts you saw.
>   – Meia

Listening anxiously to all the sounds in the house, I waited for another email to come back. Less than a minute later, I was opening his reply.

Meia,
I took that article off the web over ten years ago. I'm not sure why it's coming up in a search now. Finding that island was an accident, and although I did go back... I'm not at liberty to say what I found there. It was an unbelievable experience, one I will take with me for the rest of my life, but one I cannot share with a ten-year-old girl.
Sorry, Atticus

My fingers shook as I replied.

Please Mr. Atticus. I know you saw dragons. I have to know for sure they exist and I'm not crazy. Please, Atticus.

I uttered a silent prayer before I pushed send. I waited five minutes, staring at the status bar to my email. I had almost given up hope when the soft ding pierced the silence.

Meia, you can't help them. You must stay away. That's all I will say. I won't reply again. Sleep well.

My heart fluttered with relief. *You can't help them,* I read again silently.
He says I can't help them, which means something is there. Something like... a dragon.
I tiptoed back to my bed, reminding myself not to dance with glee. Snuggled under the covers, I couldn't wipe the grin plastered across my face.
The dragons were real.

Chapter Seven
DEGLAN - THE DRAGON

The darkness surrounded me as I pressed through the thick clouds. When I rose above the storm, the night stretched as far as my eye could see. I had no idea where I was going or how long it would take to get there, but the almost audible voice of the girl guided me. When I flew too far in one direction, a gentle tug in my heart directed me back on track. In the right direction, she would hum a happy tune, making me smile and helping to pass the time.

When the first rays of sun peeked their way over the horizon, I knew I needed to seek refuge soon. Flying into the sun would be a death sentence. Not only could I not see, but the first morning's light is always the most harsh.

The first island I'd found -- if you could call the small bit of earth an island at all -- was barely bigger than my dwelling back at home, but it provided me everything I needed to rest. I'd always heard learning to fly was hard work, but I had no idea it would take every ounce of my strength. I curled under one of the few trees on the island and slept, only rising when I could sit up without falling over again. I blinked at the mid-morning sun, high in the sky above the waters.

Could I have slept for a full day and night? The growl in my stomach confirmed my suspicions.

The tree I'd been sleeping under had fruit that looked like peaches on its limbs. I plucked one and sniffed the outside. The sweet smell of nectar filled my nostrils and I gobbled the fruit whole. I picked several more from the wild tree, thinking it was odd for it to be growing in such an obscure place.

I wandered around the island and found a small pool of fresh water collected in a deep rock. I slurped it up, thankful the rains had supplied me with a cool drink.

The sun had begun its descent across the sky by the time the voice called me again. She urged me on and I took to the sky at once. Her voice was more distinct and definitely louder as I got closer to wherever she was leading me.

Another storm brewed directly in my path. I debated going around, but every time I veered off course, the voice lured me back.

Determination raced through my veins with the feeling that I was close. I flew into the torrential rains, hoping to rise above the clouds. But each time I'd broken through what I thought was the top, another gray mass gathered above. Instead of fighting the storm, I traveled blindly through the mess of rain and wind, water clinging to every part of my body and making my flight even harder.

It felt like I'd been flying through the monstrous storm for hours before the clouds parted and the moonlit horizon rose in front of me. Light bounced off the foamy waters and a school of dolphins shot up, headed the same direction I was.

Her excited voice echoed in my mind, telling me I was almost there. I gazed across the beautiful ocean, proud of the things I'd already accomplished. If someone would've told me two days earlier I'd fly alone on a journey into the unknown, I would've said they were out of their mind. This certainly wasn't something I would've chosen to do. But I wasn't alone. She was with me… whoever she was.

There was no warning when my wings wobbled with exhaustion. Instead of one moon, two now wiggled in the sky. I needed to find shelter quickly. I shook my head and from the corner of my eye caught a glimpse of land. I veered towards it, my head pounding with fatigue. I tried to steady my flight but still slammed into the sand at full speed, tumbling head over tail for at least three hundred feet. Pain shot through every part of my body. I wanted to just lay there, but I knew I had to seek better cover.

I pulled myself to all fours and crawled toward the trees. I'd only gone about a hundred feet before I collapsed, head hitting the sand with a thump. I didn't bother taking my backpack off, I just wanted to rest. At least for a little while.

Chapter Eight
MEIA - THE HUMAN

All night my dreams startled me awake. I must've had at least ten dreams in the eight hours I tried to sleep. All of them were different from any I'd had before. Instead of the dragon needing help, I called for him and he followed. It was as if we were playing hide-and-go-seek all over the ocean. By morning, I was a zombie as I got ready for school. Fortunately, it was Friday and I would be able to sleep in tomorrow if the same dreams woke me. I checked the internet before I headed for the shower. The connection had expired sometime during the night.

My familiar bowl of oatmeal was set in front of me at the breakfast table. I loved a hot breakfast, and oatmeal was one of my favorites. I sprinkled some sugar, then poured in the milk. Inside my bowl, the familiar shape of an atoll appeared. I moved the rolled oats around and made it an amoeba shape, like Penrhyn.

As I stared at my bowl, my mind darted to the Atticus' dragon island. Had Penrhyn been one of the islands I played hide-and-go-seek on last night in my dreams? I couldn't remember. All I could remember was that my blue dragon was there and I was with him.

"Whatcha doing, Meia?" Mrs. Bensen sat at the table with her coffee. "Looks like an atoll in your bowl," she mused.

"Yeah, it's Penrhyn," I said, without caring if she thought I was crazy for making my breakfast into a Cook Island. Even though I'd only been with the Bensens a couple of months, they had already proved mostly immune to my outbreaks. Most of the time, it didn't faze them. I looked up from my bowl, remembering the conversation I'd overhead about a new placement. Had I been too weird?

"That's cool. So the Cook Islands raised your interest?"

"Yeah, I even dreamed about them all last night, though I kept waking up after each dream ended."

"I thought you were acting a little weird today. You want to stay home and rest?"

My mouth hung open in shock. Was Mrs. Bensen really telling me I could stay home and sleep? This was too good to be true.

"I..." Visions of a math test flashed through my head and made me groan. "There's only a week left of school, I should probably go." I hesitated a moment, remembering she had indeed called me weird. "Mrs. Bensen, do you think I'm *too* weird?"

"What? No, that isn't what I meant. You're just not your normal, talkative self. You usually share your dreams with me and you didn't this morning. But I see it's because you dreamed of the Cook Islands instead. That's quite a change from your dragon dreams."

"Well... the dragon was there too." I bit my lip and met her expectant eyes. I tilted my head when a realization came. "I think I've always dreamed about him in the Cook Islands; I just didn't know they were an actual place."

"That's peculiar," Mrs. Bensen said, sipping her coffee. Her left eyebrow rose curiously as she put down her cup.

"Mrs. Bensen?" I moved my oatmeal around my bowl again. "Are you looking for another placement for me?" I didn't want to look up and meet her eyes. I knew how hard it was for my previous foster parents to come out and say it, yet here I was asking.

"Meia, of course not. What made you think that?"

"I overheard you last week on the phone," I said, daring to look up.

"I'm not sure what you overheard, but we most certainly aren't seeking a new placement for you. Are you happy here?" Her eyes were sad, but filled with the care she'd always given.

"I'm happy, Mrs. Bensen. I really am. I worry you will get sick of my dragon talk... and me."

"Oh, honey," she said, and reached across the table to pat my hand. "You're already precious to us. I was talking to your social worker recently, but not for any reason you'd think." She hesitated and withdrew her hand from mine. "We want to go on a trip and... well, we wanted to make sure you could join us before we said anything to you."

"Really? Where are we going?"

"Where do you want to go?" she asked with a twinkle in her eye.

Visions of atolls flashed in my mind. It was farfetched, but she had asked.

"I would love to go to the Cook Islands."

"Okay," she said, then leaned back in her chair, still grinning.

"W-w-what?" I sat up and looked at her in disbelief. My heart stammered at the same rhythm my mouth had.

Mr. Bensen waltzed into the kitchen wearing a wide grin. "I see she broke the news."

"For real? We're going to the Cook Islands?"

The two exchanged looks then laughed.

"You want to go to the Cook Islands? Fine, let's go."

"We're going just like that?" I could hardly believe what they were saying.

"Well, to be perfectly honest," Mrs. Bensen said, with a quick glance at Mr. Bensen, "we'd been planning this trip for a while. It's why you overheard me talking to your social worker; we had to okay the trip out of the country."

"So you planted the thought of the Cook Islands in my head on purpose?" I asked Mr. Bensen, knowing he might have. Although, it still wouldn't explain why I'd been dreaming about them for so long.

"Yes, and it worked, because now you want to go."

"When do we leave?"

"Next week, after you get out of school." Mrs. Bensen couldn't wipe the smile from her face.

"What? Really?" I bounced up and down on the chair. "But what about passports and stuff?"

"You already have a passport from when you were younger."

"I do?"

She nodded. "It arrived yesterday from your social worker."

I fell back into my chair, unable to believe I was going to the Cook Islands. It wasn't the dragon island, but it was close enough for my daydreams to take over from there.

Chapter Nine
DEGLAN · THE DRAGON

The sun crested the thick canopy of trees, skewering me with beams of harsh afternoon light. I swiveled around and realized I had somehow wedged myself between two trees with barely enough room to wiggle my way out. My mind was hazy, but I was sure when I passed out, there had been plenty of room between me and the nearest tree... unless.

I raced to the crystal-clear blue water that collected in a tide pool near the shore. I gathered my nerve and peered over the side of the mirrored water. I gazed at the unfamiliar reflection and cringed. I'd heard terrible things about the end of the ninth year, but this was ridiculous. Born with two horns, I now had several more jutting from the top of my dark blue head and running the length of my body. They were hideous and at the moment looked like a row of incisors had sprung out of my head overnight. I leaned closer, checking their length with my claw and shook my head in disbelief. My claws were huge, definitely not the same size as when I'd left the island last night. I twisted my head and stared at the face that gawked back at me. I growled at my reflection and blinked hard a few times when I saw my enormous teeth. If I wasn't mistaken, I was the largest dragon I'd ever seen.

I sucked in a breath, bringing myself up to full height, knowing this supernatural transformation from a hatchling to full-grown dragon somehow skipped the adolescent step. I whipped my tail so quickly that I smacked into a tree and coconuts toppled down like hail. Birds of all kinds took off into the sky, retreating from my presence. I stretched my massive wings, bumping another nearby tree, sending the last curious bird fluttering away. The thin membranes between each bone in my wings were laced with blue veins of power.

My throat was dry, and I realized more smoke trailed from my nostrils than normal. I knew I could control the smoke, but at the moment I was proud to see it rise into the air. It was a symbol of power and prestige with the dragons; the thicker the smoke, the cooler the dragon. However, the length of the fire stood out beyond anything.

I searched the area to make sure I was alone, then inhaled deeply with my eyes closed. I raised my head to the sky, so I wouldn't catch anything afire, and blew. The fire from my lungs burst over my pursed lips, and I emitted a massive growl I hadn't intended. The fire shot high in the air, scorching the nearby palm trees. The leaves recoiled, running from the blistering heat. I watched in awe as the flames danced higher and higher with each recurrent breath. I only stopped displaying my impressive fire when some shreds of old leaves on a nearby palm tree caught fire. I slurped up water and spewed it at the tree, dousing the flames.

I grinned at this new ability, knowing my fire could reach further than any I'd seen before. Maybe I *was* the dragon from the legend, which was why Lord Edric wanted me gone. My mark tingled as if to confirm the thoughts roaming across my mind. No one could deny the mark was a dragon with its body curled, eyes peering out from my blue scales. I flexed my arm and pushed the tingling sensation away, the thought of leaving my parents still too raw on my mind to feel happy about what any of this might mean.

Struggling with the now tiny leather pack, I pulled open the clasp and dug out some food. I ripped through the dried meat, knowing if my mom had been watching I would have been scolded for how savagely I ate. I knew I should probably hunt, but I hadn't been taught how to hunt properly yet. Usually, dragons learned in their fifteenth year. It's probably a basic instinct they repress us from following until they know we can control ourselves. I knew there had been times I wanted to rip into a smaller creature for no other reason than my hunger. I never did it because it was frowned upon. The clan had hunters, and unless your job was to hunt you didn't do it. However, I wasn't on Teken Island anymore, and my rations wouldn't last long before I would starve. Maybe my instincts would kick in when I needed them most. I gobbled the dried meat in my claw and told myself I would hunt when I was hungry again.

After a long drink from the fresh water, I decided it was time to explore the island to see if it could be a place of sanctuary while I decided what to do next. The girl from my dreams had led me here, but now what? Did I wait for her? Or did I continue traveling until I found her?

The half-burned palm tree marked the spot where I hid my pack in the leaves. I debated taking it along on my exploration, but even on the loosest setting, the straps were too tight now. If I ran into danger, it would get in my way.

I picked my way through the dense trees, listening for anything other than the caw of the birds or scurry of my cousin, the lizard, underfoot. I stepped into the open and gazed at the beautiful blue water of the familiar ocean. A school of dolphins shot out of the water off the coast, then disappeared again. The beach stretched close to a league on either side of me.

I could've taken a small flight around the island, but that worried me in the light of day. I wasn't sure who or what resided there, and I didn't want to make myself a target. At least, not yet. I might have been bigger than I'd been on Teken Island, but I was only ten and something bigger could be out there hiding beneath the trees.

I heard a rustle in the trees to my left. Frozen in fear, my heart pounded in my throat as I stared at the branches swaying back and forth under the pressure of whatever tried to push its way behind them.

When underbrush parted, I gasped.

Chapter Ten
MEIA - THE HUMAN

The next week passed in a blur. Cate was jealous the Bensens were taking me on a tropical vacation, but I promised to send her a postcard or seventeen giving her every detail.

The humid tropical air greeted me when I stepped off the plane on Roratonga, the main Cook Island.

When my feet hit the ground, euphoria rushed over me. I wanted to start exploring immediately. However, jetlag was real, and when they convinced me to lie down, I crashed and slept until morning.

The early morning sunlight pricked my eyelids, interrupting the dreams of my dragon. I scrambled to my feet and rushed around the hotel room, readying myself for our first day's adventure. We boarded the chartered plane for Penrhyn, the closest island to where Atticus had seen the dragons. I could barely stay in my seat as the plane flew over the beautiful atolls. I recognized each as we passed, which surprised Mrs. Bensen. When we landed, it was all I could do to not shove my way off the plane.

The bright, cloudless sky and the water met at the horizon, making it hard to tell which ended where. I watched the waves roll softly to the beach and marveled at their beauty. I felt as if I was in a dream... the only difference was my dreams included a dragon.

When my feet dug into the warm sand on the beach next to the landing strip, energy rushed through my bare toes. I sensed *they* were close.

Our guide led the group to a small wooden hut with a sea turtle painted on the side. Everyone collected snorkel gear to explore the coral reefs. Mr. Bensen told me the reefs of Penrhyn had the largest variety of ocean life in all the Cook Island atolls and missing them would be a travesty... whatever that meant.

The instructor explained all the details of how to use a snorkel and mask. I thought I had it pretty much under control until I put my face in the water. No matter how hard I tried, I felt as if I was suffocating under the two inches of water we practiced in. My heart raced each time I submerged my face, and by the time they were ready to go further out I was in full panic mode. I held the mask in a death grip as the ice-cold dread caused my heart to flutter in uncomfortable intervals.

"I can't do it," I explained to Mr. Bensen. "I feel like I can't breathe underwater, and it's freaking me out. Can I stay on the beach and look for sand dollars or something?" I clasped my hands together and pleaded with him.

His eyes clouded with concern. "We don't have to go, Meia." He looked over at Mrs. Bensen, who stood with the others receiving final instructions.

"No, please go. I'll be fine. I love the beach. I'll build a sand castle or something."

Mrs. Bensen splashed over to where we stood in the water. I knew water wasn't my thing, but I had no idea I would get this panicked over putting my face in.

"Are you sure, Meia? I can stay with you..."

"No, I'll be fine. I'll stay here on the beach and explore the solid ground. Take lots of pictures of the fish and coral," I said in the most chipper voice I could muster.

The Bensens glanced between each other and reluctantly agreed, telling me to stay within sight of the snorkel shack. The instructor said something to the attendant and motioned at me, no doubt making her aware that I stayed behind.

I stood on the beach, my freshly painted toes touching the rippling water, encircled by the sun that bounced in rainbows off the waves. The snorkelers faded out across the reef where all I could see were the little spouts of water, like whale blowholes going off now and then.

"You scared of water?" the woman behind the counter asked in her thick accent when I handed her my mask and snorkel.

"Yeah, I guess." I knew it was more than that, but I wasn't about to debate it with a stranger. "I'm going to look for shells," I said, motioning at the beach.

The attendant nodded, and her braids bobbed in unison. "Go play. You need sometang, you jus` ask Betta here."

I walked with one foot in the water and one on the moist sand. Broken white shells dotted the shore with a few bits of jellyfish and seaweed mixed around. I knelt, plucked a piece of blue shell from its shallow grave, then rinsed it in the warm water. The shell was transparent in the sun, and when I held it toward the ocean, it captured the bouncing rainbows off the water. I slipped it into my pocket and searched the beach for more buried treasure. Movement in the sand near my toes caused me to jump back in alarm. I peered closer when a shell made its way towards a large rock. The claw of a hermit crab jabbed out of the shell and swiped something on the beach, then continued to lug its shell up and over his obstacle. I watched as it neared the top of the rock and paused, poking its head and body from the shell to bask in the sun.

A loud crash echoed from the trees behind me. I spun on my heels and saw birds fluttering to the sky. Gooseflesh rose on my arms as the birds scattered in all directions. I looked toward the shack to be sure the woman wasn't watching, then against my better judgment I scurried into the trees. The temperature dropped drastically, sending a shiver racing through my body.

THUNK.

The sound reverberated in front of me, stopping me in my tracks. The squawk of a bird overhead made me stumble backward into a tree. I grasped at it to keep myself upright as fear raced through my veins. Darting into the trees suddenly felt like a bad idea. I scanned my surroundings for movement and debated my best escape route. When another noise pierced the silence, all reasoning left and I dashed back the way I thought I'd come. I pushed my way through the brush and back onto the beach, but the snorkel shack was nowhere. I headed back into the trees, remembering the lagoon in the middle, thinking I must have been turned around.

I made my way out onto another portion of beach. Panic overtook me when the snorkel shack was still nowhere in sight. My hands shook as I headed back through the brush.

A deep growl penetrated my consciousness and paralyzed me with fear. My breath came in ragged pants as I listened for the animal. The trees swayed in large awkward motions in front of me. I jumped behind the nearest tree and fell to my knees, my forehead pressed to the ground, and hands clasped protectively over my head as I'd been taught in a tornado drill. However, I knew no tornado would growl like that.

Deep, horrible breathing echoed and the smell of singed plants hung in the air. I waited for what seemed like a lifetime, listening and praying for whatever it was to leave me alone. When the birds returned to their loud chirping, I lifted my head and checked the area, but saw nothing. My heart pounded in my chest as I crept forward on my knees, intending to exit the trees again.

Dry leaves crackled under me as I scrambled to my feet and hurried toward the beach. The sparkle of water peeked through the trees ahead. I could have found a thinner bit of trees, but I wanted out. I leaned into the underbrush, forcing a path through the dense cover. The branches scratched at my flesh, sending stings of pain shooting down my arms and legs.

A beach appeared, vacant and unfamiliar. I looked up and down the shoreline and saw nothing. I sat in the warm sand and buried my head in my knees. The tears stung my eyes, but I refused to let them fall. I knew I should sit tight and someone would find me. All the survival guides said so.

I scooped some sand and watched it fall through my fingers. I tried to focus on the cool of the sand to calm my nerves.

I brushed the sand stuck to my legs, stopping when I got to my ankle. The smooth line of a scar gleamed white in the sun. I traced the raised skin with my finger, wondering once again where I'd gotten it. The only mention of it in my records was that it existed, not how it was caused.

The sparkle of another blue shell caught my attention. I leaned forward to grab it, but paused when my hand fell into a large print. I traced the deep, moist print, then realized they were all around me. They ended near the water's edge. As I stared at it, something moved in front of me. I squinted, wondering if it was a hermit crab. When it moved again, I jumped to my feet. The sand stirred ten feet from me. My eyes bobbed from side to side, scanning the beach for my getaway. Either something very large was about to pop out from the ground or my mind was playing mammoth tricks on me.

The hairs on the back of my neck stood up in alarm. Someone or something was watching me. Terror rolled through my chest, tightening with each forced breath. I needed to run... now.

My feet were in motion before my head realized that they needed to be moving, which probably made me look like a baby taking her first steps. Before I could get far, I tripped and crashed headfirst into the sand. I pushed off the ground sputtering salty sand from my tongue. The sand shifted near my face and I screamed. I rolled away and prepared to dart again, when the voice of a boy stopped me.

"Wait. Don't run."

On my feet, I searched for the boy, wanting to grab him and save us both from whatever was about to pop up.

"Quick! Come out of the bushes! There's something..." I let my words die on my tongue as the sand stirred again in front of me. "What the... Who's there?"

There was a short pause and I heard a sigh.

"It's me. Deglan."

I tilted my head toward the voice, seemingly coming from the sky but saw nothing. "Who? Where are you? Why can't I see you?" I looked down the beach for some sign confirming I hadn't gone crazy. Some boy was having a laugh at my expense… and an American boy at that. "Were you the one stirring the sand?" My fear turned quickly into annoyance.

"You can't see me?"

"No, I can't see you if you're hiding."

"I'm standing a few paces in front of you."

"What?" I stepped back, looking for some hidden mirrors or spy gear some geek kid thought was a good show. I could feel my blood beginning to boil. This might be why foster families wouldn't keep me. *Doesn't play well with others* was probably written right under *has dragon nightmares.* "Good one. I still don't see you." As the words rolled off my tongue, my breath caught in my throat.

A low grumble echoed in my ears as more sand moved toward me. I jumped and stumbled backward, then scrambled to my feet again. Maybe he was a master illusionist, but he was freaking me out.

"Don't be afraid."

"Yeah, that's pretty easy for you to say. You aren't talking to…Why can't I see you?" My heart played ping-pong with my chest. I didn't know if I should be afraid or really annoyed.

"I think I have to give you something for you to see me."

I shivered as a warm gust of air moved my hair across my face. I tapped my foot, trying to decide what sort of illusion this was. "Okay, fine. I'll play along. What do you want to give me?"

"Hold out your hand, and you may want to close your eyes."

"What? Why?" This was getting old quick.

"Because… I'm… different from you. I… don't want you

to be afraid if you can see me."

"Okay, fine, but I'm going to count to ten, and if I don't see you when I reopen my eyes I'm done and going back to the normal side of the island."

"Deal," the timid voice spoke again. "Close your eyes."

"They're closed, and my hand is out in case you can't tell. Now, I'm going to start counting. One... two..." Something cold touched my palm.

"Don't open them yet... give me a minute."

"Three... four... five..." I continued counting, not impressed. For all I knew he had placed a slug in my open palm. "Eight... nine... ten. Okay, I'm opening my eyes now, and this better be good."

Fortunately, the gift wasn't a slug. Instead, it was a small piece of blue shell no larger than a silver dollar, much like the one I'd found on the beach earlier.

"Okay, so... uh... thanks for the shell, but I still don't see you." I glanced down the beach again.

"I'm hiding now. I think you need to be prepared for what you see next."

"And what will I see next?" I said, trying not to sound as irritated as I felt.

"That isn't a shell," he said in a soft, even tone. "It's a scale."

"Eww. Like a fish scale?" I said, holding the scale between my thumb and pointer like it had cooties.

"No, it's not a fish scale. It's one of *my* scales."

"Your scales?" I turned it over in my hand, understanding hitting me like a blast of arctic air. "You mean...?" My voice quivered as butterflies danced in my insides. "What are you?" The words escaped my lips in barely a whisper.

"I think *you* know what I am."

"A dragon," I managed breathlessly, unable to break my gaze from the scale.

"Yes, a dragon."

I turned toward his voice, the fear melting away to

excitement. "I knew you were real!" I wanted to jump up and down. My dreams were true; a dragon stood five feet from me, hidden in the trees. "I want to see you. Can I see you?" My heart raced.

He released a nervous laugh. Pale yellow eyes glowed in the cover of the trees. I held my breath, ready for him to come onto the beach.

"MEIA!"

I whipped around. Mrs. Bensen ran frantically down the beach. When I looked back, Deglan was gone.

Chapter Eleven
DEGLAN · THE DRAGON

My heart thudded against my chest as I hid behind the mass of trees. Meia. Her name was Meia, and she was the face from my dream. I pulled her voice toward me through the wind and heard the conversation clearly.

"Meia, are you okay?" said the voice of a frantic, older woman.

"Yeah, I'm fine. I was looking for shells. I didn't realize I'd wandered so far down the beach."

"When I looked up and didn't see you, I panicked." The woman's elevated tone dropped a few notches. "I know it's a small island, but you still need to be careful."

"I'm sorry I worried you, Mrs. Bensen."

I scrambled toward the edge of the trees as quiet and fast as I could. I peeked through, hoping to catch a glimpse of Meia before she disappeared. She walked shoulder-to-shoulder with the other woman, turned once to survey where we'd been standing, then disappeared behind the bend.

What does this mean? How did my father know I would find her? Is there more to the legend than even I know? And how come she was so surprised if she was the one who beckoned me here? The questions swarmed my mind like fruit flies on a rotting banana.

Deglan. Meia's voice spoke into my mind. *The dragon from my dreams is Deglan.* I looked around, confused that I heard her voice in my head. *I have to get back to him. I have to find out if I can help.*

Help? How does she know I need help?

Deglan? Her voice questioned in my head.

I scrambled toward the bend to see her again.

Deglan? The way she called, it sounded like she expected me to respond. She walked toward a human emerging from the water.

I concentrated on her and thought my reply. *Meia? Can... can you hear me?*

Meia turned and stared at the exact spot I hid. *Yes, I can hear you, but... how can I hear you?*

I don't know. Somehow, we've created a link between our minds.

I focused on Meia, and even from this distance, my dragon eyes could make out her exact movements. When the woman prompted her to turn again, she tucked her hand behind her back and played with the scale between her thumb and forefinger.

Maybe the scale created the link. But even as the words rolled out of my mind, I knew it had to be something larger than that. Something deeper and maybe even connected to Teken Island. I brushed the thought away, thinking that was impossible.

Meia sat on a bench near the brown turtle dwelling as the others returned to the water with strange contraptions tied to their heads. When they disappeared under the water, I panicked until their blowholes spouted over the waving waters.

Deglan, are you there? Her voice rang though the silence.

I'm here, hiding in the bushes around the bend.

Meia turned her head my direction. *I don't see you.*

I think it's best that way. I don't want to call attention to myself.

Are you... really a dragon? Is this for real? Am I dreaming? It wouldn't be the first time!

No Meia, it's not a dream.

She swiveled on the seat to face me. *Have you been dreaming about me, like I've been dreaming about you?*

I only just dreamed of you two nights ago. In the dream,

you told me to flee, then led me to this island.

You're in danger aren't you?

The way she asked, I knew she was confirming what she already knew.

You didn't happen to dream about why I would be in danger... did you? I asked, creeping forward in the trees and resting my head on the sand. My snout stuck out enough that if she knew what she was looking for she would surely see me.

No, not really. You were always running from other dragons, but I never knew why, only that you were in danger. I felt so connected to you that I'd wake up screaming, frantic to find you and help. But then realize it was only a dream. Besides, dragons are a myth.

I grinned at her last admission. *I'm not a myth.*

Can you come closer, so I can see if you're truly the same dragon from my dreams?

I lifted my head off the sand and stared into her face as she searched the trees for an answer. If we'd met yesterday, I would have been the same size as she was, maybe a head taller. But today, I was at least four times her size, and the thought of showing myself frightened me. What if she were terrified? What if she ran and I never saw her again? The ache in my chest told me that couldn't happen.

I don't know, Meia. I'm afraid I'll scare you. I'm much bigger than I was even yesterday. I've grown since I left my island. And not just a little, either, I'm much taller than your human companions. I don't want you to be afraid of me. I wanted to continue in my thoughts and tell her my soul longed for her friendship, but I stopped.

You won't scare me Deglan. I've been dreaming about dragons... about you... for as long as I can remember. She looked from me to the woman who poked her head from the water and waved.

I took a deep breath, then crept to the edge of the trees, careful not to disturb the vegetation or call attention to myself. Mere paces behind Meia, I stopped and crouched in the brush again.

You have to promise you won't scream.

I won't scream. I promise.

I held my breath, lifted my body to its full height, and lightly pushed my way through the trees. Meia's eyes lit up when they connected with mine and I grinned.

Chapter Twelve
MEIA - THE HUMAN

My mouth hung open in shock when the blue dragon from my dreams stood ten feet from me. I didn't want to scream. The thought of laughing or dancing came to my mind, but not screaming. It was him — it was really him.

He was humongous and beautiful. His iridescent scales, stacked one on top of the other over his navy blue skin, sparkled in the afternoon sun. The large slits in the middle of his pale yellow eyes moved when he blinked. Horns stuck over the top of his head and ran down his back. Tucked behind his front legs were what I assumed to be his wings, boney and jutting out oddly from his sides. His pointed ears stuck out from either side of his head, twitching, as he stood frozen.

Is he afraid of me?

He was huge but his posture told me he couldn't be that old. He stared at the ground and faint gray smoke trailed from his nostrils. His eyes were filled with anxiety when he looked at me.

I glanced from the snorkel shack back to Deglan, thankful the braided woman wasn't sticking her nosy head out.

"How old are you?" I whispered.

"I'll be celebrating my tenth year soon."

I grinned and saw some of his worry melt away. He lifted his head and offered me a lopsided grin.

"I'm ten too," I said, then looked to the water to check the Bensens' snorkel progress.

"You're small for ten?" He cocked his head to the side and studied me.

"No, not really. I'm tall for my age; taller than most of the boys in my class. I think I'm just right... for a human. Are you... big for ten?"

"No doubt," he said and looked down again. "I've grown a lot in the last hours. I think there's something in this air or..." He hesitated and leaned down, bringing his face much closer to mine. "I wasn't this large yesterday and I know I'm much larger than most other dragons. Even the elders. Maybe the coming lunar eclipse has something to do with it."

His eyes seemed guarded as he stared into the sand, moving his claw, as if he tried to hide it.

Does she know about the mark? Deglan's voice echoed in my head.

Before I could debate speaking aloud, the words tumbled from my lips. "What mark?" Deglan's head shot up and terror flashed through his eyes. "I'm sorry. You just said..." I stepped toward him without thinking. It seemed so natural for me to be talking with a dragon. I'd almost forgotten it wasn't until he backed away.

"Oh, you heard that?" he said in his timid voice again.

I nodded. "I didn't mean to scare you. I'm struggling to understand all this as much as you are."

He pulled his right arm out from under him and twisted it toward the sun. At first, the mark on his arm looked like nothing more than a scar from a battle. But as I stared, I realized it was shaped like dragon with a red spot for its eye.

"When dragons are hatched, legend says the first specks of light to penetrate our shell form the mark you see."

I scoffed. "That is some pretty creative light."

He grinned. "Well, that's just it. This isn't the mark I was hatched with. It's been... changing a lot lately. Yesterday, it changed more than it'd changed in years and hasn't changed since."

I cautiously moved toward Deglan as he held his

forearm out toward me. "May I touch it?"

He shrugged, "I guess." His grin wrapped around his face, reaching his large yellow eyes.

The tension between us dissolved like sugar in warm tea. I stepped toward him, excitement making my movements jerky and precise. It felt as if I was sneaking into the kitchen to take the last chocolate chip cookie.

"Who you talkin' to gurl?"

I whisked around to see the braided woman's head bob out of the snorkel shack. She stared directly at me, taking no notice of the blue dragon.

"Oh... you know, talking to myself. It's something we Americans do," I said, trying to hold in the hysterics that bubbled in my belly.

"Das Americans..." her voice trailed off and she disappeared into the shack.

I covered my mouth and toppled into the sand laughing. Deglan watched with a curious expression.

"So I guess no one can see you," I said, pushing my feet into the warm sand inches from him.

"Nope. I'm surprised you can see me at all. My giving you a gift was an instruction-yard game we play back on Teken Island. I had no idea there was any truth to it."

"Can I only see you if I have the scale?"

"I don't know. It can't hurt to see what happens if you set it down."

I placed the scale on the rock beside me, and instantly he vanished. "Whoa. You're gone." I picked it up and Deglan reappeared like a magic trick.

"Interesting. I wonder..." He tapped his chin with his large claw. "Maybe, if I *give* you the scale, it won't matter."

I frowned and stood to my feet. "Didn't you already give me the scale?"

"Well," he said, plucking the scale from my fingers. The breath stuck in my throat when he disappeared. "I didn't technically give it to you; I only placed it in your hand." The air moved around me as he shuffled past. "One instruction-yard game worked, maybe this one will too." He cleared his throat and began speaking again, this time trying to sound more grown up. "Meia, this dragon scale belongs to you now." He placed the scale in my upturned palm and appeared before my eyes.

"Okay... now what?"

"I don't know. Maybe try setting it down again?"

I set the scale on the bench beside me, and when he didn't vanish, I grinned. "It worked! I can still see you."

He let out a small chuckle that sounded like a happy growl. "That's so weird. I wonder what else works that we thought were only games."

He moved into a more relaxed position with his underside on the sand and his front legs in front of him. He arched his long neck and rested it on his claw. His snout alone must have been at least as big as my torso.

A small ripple of fear coursed through my body when I returned to the bench. This dragon could gobble me up in one bite if he wanted to. I scooted away from the warm breath flowing across my toes, raised my feet to the bench, and hugged my legs.

"So now what?" I said, turning to him. His eyes watched me, the slits in his pupils changing sizes as he blinked. "What about that mark?"

"I'm not sure. We have legends that say things about a dragon with a mark..."

"And you could be that dragon?"

He shrugged. "That's why I had to leave Teken Island. Someone knew my mark had changed, and if the legends are true..." His voice trailed off as he looked out over the waves. A commotion at the shoreline to my left caught my attention; the snorkel party emerged from the water. Deglan raised his head and retreated into the bushes.

"If they can't see you, why are you hiding?" I stood, grabbed the scale from the table, and pocketed it. Regardless of if it meant anything now, it would remind me this was NOT a dream.

"Just in case," he said, disappearing among the large leaves. From where I sat, I could see the faint hint of his yellow eyes.

"Just in case? You think someone can see you?"

"There's no way to be sure without putting myself at risk. Humans are the reason we went into hiding," he said, his eyes sad and filled with worry.

"What? How did—?"

"We'll talk later."

"When?" I called into the trees, but there was no answer.

"Meia, who are you talking to?" Mr. Bensen's voice sounded from behind me.

"Oh, she jus' talkin' to daself," said the snorkel keeper, taking the gear from Mr. Bensen. "They alls like dat."

Mr. Bensen laughed and sat on the bench, flipping his hair in every direction, spraying water droplets all over me. "You missed a great dive, Kiddo. We saw some dolphins on the outside of the reef and a small shark."

"Shark?" I gave an exaggerated gulp and sat beside Mr. Bensen on the bench, wiping off my arm. "I knew there was a reason I didn't go in the water."

He laughed again as he stuck his finger in his ear and shook his head sideways. "It was the size of my hand. You should go next time. Once you realize you can breathe, it's amazing."

"I dunno," I said and allowed my gaze to drift to Deglan, still visible through the brush. "I think I'll leave the snorkeling to you and Mrs. Bensen. Water isn't my thing."

"But dragons are," he said wagging his eyebrows. His eyes darted to where Deglan stood invisible in the trees. "And dragons like water." He looked at me, winked, then rose and greeted Mrs. Bensen.

Had he known I was talking to Deglan?

Impossible.

Chapter Thirteen
DEGLAN - THE DRAGON

I watched as Meia disappeared into the distance, guided by the two humans. I wanted to follow her, but I couldn't risk revealing myself. I could tell by the look on the human man's face as his eyes traced the area I hid, he knew I was here.

I'd overheard them say they weren't leaving the island until dusk, which gave me little time to think of a plan. The thought of scooping her up and flying away crossed my mind, but that would raise too many alarms for the humans who still believed us to be myths. If I had learned anything in instruction, it was that humans would kill anything they were afraid of — meaning dragons — a harsh reminder why we've remained hidden on the cloaked island.

I stalked through the forest back to the burnt palm, hungry again, but unwilling to hunt. When I pulled open the pack, a book sat on top of my food rations. The cover was black with a brown dragon coiled in a circle in the middle. It looked vaguely familiar, but inside were ancient pages, claw-written in languages I'd never learned. Toward the center, the writing changed to words written in my own language.

My stomach twisted into knots when I recognized my mother's claw-writing. It was her diary. I sucked back the tears, remembering the look on her face when I fled, all because of my mark. Tears slowly dripping down my cheeks, I read the entry dated ten years earlier.

Lord Edric has issued a decree among the Teken: All hatchlings born with a mark shaped as a dragon must be brought to him. This has caused widespread panic throughout the land and mothers have been poking holes in the shells of their eggs in the early morning light to ensure their marks are not formed as such. Hatchlings have already been lost from this practice. My hatchling is due soon. If his mark looks like a dragon, I will not sacrifice him to this decree. I will hide him if I must.

She was talking about me. How could she have known I might bear the mark? I turned the page and stopped at the writing in my mother's claw.

Lord Edric has convinced the Teken clan that the marked hatchling must be found. He believes the dragon will upset the ways of the clan and now requires marks to be checked not only at birth, but at the lunar eclipse as part of the Rising Ceremony. Most dragons are accepting of this new practice, because none of their hatchlings bears such a mark. Harold and I believe a new era is on the horizon and it scares Lord Edric. I don't want to live in fear for the rest of our lives. I believe the dragon mark symbolizes change and I welcome it.

I flipped through and found another I could read, dated a few days after the previous. The entry turned my blood icy.

He must be stopped. Lord Edric has done something terrible. A ten-year-old hatchling whose mark changed into something resembling a dragon has disappeared. No one seems to know where he's gone and Lord Edric forbids anyone to speak of it. I'm afraid for my Deglan. Harold says I'm overreacting. Lord Edric has also discovered the foreigners are expecting a child. Rumor has it he is afraid of what a child born on his land could mean. I know the foreigners mean us no harm; they only want to live among us, learn our ways, and help us in any way they can. They don't want to see our race end. They think Lord Edric is destroying us.

Eager to read more, I turned the page and pictures fell from the binding and drifted to the ground. The first made my heart warm with a thousand rays of the sun. It was my mother with a small, blue dragon in her arms — me. Her eyes peered down at me and her expression was of the proudest dragon in the universe.

I flipped to the next one and almost dropped it back to the ground. It was similar to the first, but this time a human woman, holding a newborn wrapped in a pink blanket, joined us. I stared at the faces, wondering why my mother would have such a picture.

Humans are forbidden to the dragon's way of life. If anyone had found this...

My thoughts trailed off when the woman's eyes jumped out at me from the print. Those were Meia's eyes. Was this newborn Meia? Was this Meia's mother? I thumbed through the book, but found nothing more stuffed between the pages. I turned to the next claw-written entry.

The foreigners and their daughter left Teken Island today under the cover of night. It was difficult to let them go, but it's for their safety and ours. Lord Edric discovered that their child was born upon our land, and he threatened their lives and the lives of anyone who harbored them. No one knows we befriended them, and before they left, Harold gave the child a Dragon's Promise of safety from other dragons. She has the mark of our undying protection. Let Lord Edric get around that.

If this was indeed Meia, then she was born on Teken Island, which might explain our link. Our parents were friends and their protection still resides over Meia's life. A

Dragon's Promise is like a tattoo on one's soul, though I'd never heard of anyone giving a Promise to a human.

Why hadn't my parents told me about these humans, and who were the people with Meia today? The woman's face wasn't the one in the picture.

I tossed the book into my pack. The thought of Lord Edric purposefully attacking innocent humans tied my stomach into knots. I needed to discuss my findings with Meia.

Meia? Can you hear me from where you are? I asked, testing the link.

Yes, Deglan, I can hear you, came her happily surprised response.

We need to talk again... I hesitated, not knowing how much to share with her. *Can we meet again sometime today?*

Silence. I debated calling out again when her anxious reply shot through my mind.

I don't know. I think Mr. Bensen suspects something. I'm not sure how to slip away.

Mr. Bensen... is that the male human? I had the feeling he sensed my presence, but I didn't give him anything... unless another has. Could Meia's Mr. Bensen also have been to Teken Island? At this point, I knew anything was possible. *Meia, he might have already come into contact with a dragon. Can you ask him?*

Ask him? How exactly should I do that?

I sensed her annoyance, but she was right. If they believed us to be myths, how could she ask without looking like a complete lunatic? However, if he did know, he would realize she could see me too. The more I debated it, the more I realized she needed to find the truth. What was the worst that could happen? He could remove her from the island... and I would follow.

Chapter Fourteen
MEIA - THE HUMAN

My plate was nearly empty when Deglan's voice pierced my thoughts, requesting me to speak with Mr. Bensen. My foster parents talked casually as I debated on how to approach the subject. If I asked Mr. Bensen and he'd seen something, I had nothing to worry about. However, if he hadn't... I groaned.

"Meia, are you okay?" Mrs. Bensen asked, wiping her hands on her napkin.

"Yeah, I'm fine."

"That wasn't very convincing," she said, then rubbed my arm. "You want another Coke?" She picked up my can and shook it.

"Can I have another?" This was my chance. With her away from the table, I could question Mr. Bensen without feeling as if I were being analyzed from both sides.

"Sure you can; we're on vacation." She pushed herself from the table, wove through the crowd, and stood in the short line at the counter, out of earshot.

I took a breath and said a silent prayer. *Here goes nothing.*

"Mr. Bensen, did you see anything in the trees near the snorkel shack?"

Mr. Bensen paused mid-bite and his eyebrows furrowed.

I cleared my throat, wishing I hadn't asked.

"What do you mean, Meia? Did you see something?" The way he asked, I knew he was fishing for more information. He'd seen something in the trees; I was almost sure of it.

"I did see something," I said, and looked from his expectant eyes down to my plate. "It was a huge something." I met his eyes again. "A big, blue, enormous something."

His eyes never left mine, but he didn't say a word. I wished I could read his mind, so I would know why his eyebrows now bobbed up and down.

"Here's your Coke," Mrs. Bensen said, setting the red can on the table in front of me.

"Thanks." I forced my eyes to the can and used my thumb to press the tab. It popped open with a hiss.

"Grace." Mr. Bensen addressed Mrs. Bensen by her first name. He never used her first name. His eyes were still fixed on me, which made me uneasy. Mrs. Bensen glanced between my nervous expression and his face.

"What's wrong?"

"She saw him."

"What? What are you talking about—" Her words froze on her tongue.

She turned her gaze upon me, with what I could only describe as shock. No one said anything for minutes, all of us just staring between one another until the tour guide rang the bell, startling us to our feet. We threw our trash away and headed for the small group collecting in front of the cabana. Mr. and Mrs. Bensen held hands and exchanged nervous looks. I didn't know what it meant, but it couldn't be good. I felt as if I was in trouble, yet I hadn't done anything. Maybe if I dropped it, we could just forget I'd ever asked.

However, even as I tried to convince myself to forget about it, Mr. Bensen's words rolled through my head. *She saw him.* He had to have seen Deglan, which meant he had to have encountered dragons before. It was silly; why was I afraid? He obviously knew what I was talking about, even if he was unwilling to admit it.

"Mr. Chuv?" Mr. Bensen said to the tour guide. "What time does the flight back leave?"

"Eight-tirty, Mista Bensen."

"Wonderful. We'll meet you at the airstrip at that time.

My family and I want to walk the beach instead of taking the guided tour."

"Very well, Mista Bensen," Chuv said, gathering the others as we walked away.

No one spoke until we were away from the group, then we all started at the same time. Mr. Bensen held up his hands to silence us as he continued.

"Where is he?"

"Who?" I asked, unsure if I should give away Deglan's location.

"The dragon, Meia," he said, exasperated. I'd never seen him like this before and it worried me.

"I... I don't know," I managed through my parted lips.

"Gabriel, you're scaring her." Mrs. Bensen took my hand as we continued down the beach.

"Grace, we need to know where he is... We need to..." He trailed off and looked into the nearby trees.

I spun my head and I gasped. Deglan stood at full height just outside the tree cover. I didn't know what Mr. Bensen intended, but I took off in a sprint toward Deglan.

"Meia!" both called after me.

I ran as hard as I could and stood protectively in front of him with my arms outstretched, drawing deep breaths. I didn't know what had come over me. It wasn't as if I could do anything to help him; it would most likely be the other way around.

"Meia, it's okay," Deglan said, nudging my head with his snout. "They're friends." He tipped his head in a graceful bow toward Mr. and Mrs. Bensen, who drew near.

"What? How do you know...?" I still held my arms outstretched in a suspicious pose.

Mr. Bensen gave a deep bow when he stood in front of Deglan. My head swam with questions, but none of them left my lips. Instead, I watched them stare at one another. Mr. Bensen's eyebrows bobbed up and down again, and I realized he was speaking silently to Deglan.

"Deglan," Mr. Bensen said in greeting, as if he'd been

introduced to him thousands of times before.

How could he see him? How could he talk with him silently? What was going on? And was it my imagination, or had Deglan grown even bigger since the last time I saw him?

Chapter Fifteen
DEGLAN - THE DRAGON

"Deglan," Mr. Bensen addressed me. Just from that simple word, I knew he understand everything I'd already shared with him in the silent moment.

I bowed again and my eyes landed on Meia's shocked face. I pinched my lips together, trying not to laugh at the fact she looked like she was about to explode.

"What's going on?" Meia stomped her feet and balled her fists. "How can you see him?"

Mrs. Bensen reached her arms toward Meia, "Let us explain."

"They're friends," I said, hesitating long enough that Mr. Bensen continued.

"We've helped the dragons in the past and have been called to do it again," Mr. Bensen said, stepping forward.

I could tell Meia struggled with understanding how they even accepted that they were talking to a dragon. If what Mr. Bensen said to me silently was true, Meia's world was about to be turned upside down.

"Our connection to the dragons is far greater than you can imagine, Meia." Mr. Bensen said.

Mrs. Bensen kneeled before Meia in the sand and took her hands, looking her in the eyes. "Meia, we searched for you. It was no mistake you were placed in our care. We've known you were linked to the dragons since the day we met you."

"How could you have known I was linked to dragons?"

"Your Dragon's Promise," I said in a proud tone. "My father gave you a promise of protection before you left our island."

"Before I left? I've been there?" Her words spilled out in

complete disbelief.

"You were born there," I said in a soft tone.

Meia's mouth fell open but no sound came out.

"Our parents were friends. My mother wrote about them in her diary. I even found a picture of us together. It must be how we're linked."

"Your parents knew my parents?" Her voice broke.

"Yes, Deglan's parents are the reason you're alive," Mr. Bensen said. "Your parents were attacked when they fled the island. The dragons left you for dead in the boat. These dragons couldn't harm you, because of the Dragon's Promise, but the elements could."

"How did I get from there...?"

"Another clan of dragons found you," Mrs. Bensen cut in. "A rival clan of the Teken. Knowing they left you to die was a good enough reason to keep you alive, so they did. They had no idea—"

"—how special you were," Mr. Bensen finished.

Even from behind, I could tell Meia cried. I wanted to pick her up in my arms and hug her. Instead, I leaned down and pressed my nose into her back. She turned, her tear-stained face eye level with mine. I nuzzled my snout into her chest until she wrapped her arms around it and embraced me.

"I'm so sorry," I said.

Her tears ran down her cheeks and onto my muzzle as she held me tight.

It wasn't my fault her parents had died, but it *was* Lord Edric's. It was also because of him I had to flee my own island, and hatchlings were being sacrificed. He was the reason tears fell from her eyes. The anger boiled in me like lava from a waking volcano.

"Deglan?" The raspy words of Mr. Bensen broke the silence. "What's wrong?"

Meia backed away, her eyes bulging as she looked at me.

"What?" I said, wondering why they had odd

expressions on their faces.

"Your eyes just went from yellow to red, then back again. What were you thinking about?"

"Lord Edric..." I felt the anger bubbling again at the mention of his name.

Mrs. Bensen eyes never left mine and her voice tumbled through her barely parted lips. "It *is* him."

"I'm who?" I looked to Mr. Bensen for help.

"Mr. Bensen?" Meia said when he didn't respond.

He merely studied me, nodding his head.

Chapter Sixteen
MEIA - THE HUMAN

The whole previous hour of my life had been exciting, terrible, confusing, emotional, and I'm sure many other things I couldn't even put into words. I'd always known my connection to dragons was real. I just never considered I would be *this* connected.

It was an eerie feeling to discover I had been born on a dragon island then left for dead.

Why would a clan of dragons keep me alive just because the other wanted me dead? And how did the Bensens figure into all of this?

Questions rolled around in my head as we flew back to Rarotonga. It took a lot of convincing for me to step on the plane and leave Deglan hiding in the trees, but they told me he would meet us in the morning. If I hadn't been able to link minds, I might have jumped out of the plane with or without a parachute to get back to him. I know he would have caught me.

I sighed as I stared into the cover of night. Something had happened in those quiet moments when I held Deglan between my arms. I couldn't explain it if I tried, but I felt perfectly at peace when I touched him. My fears melted away.

Something outside the window flashed in the moonlight and I smiled when Deglan appeared with outstretched wings. He winked, then disappeared. He *would* be there when we arrived.

Mr. and Mrs. Bensen had been quiet the remainder of the night, speaking among themselves and brushing off any questions I threw their way. I should have been annoyed, but somehow all my years of wondering had ended and with it came a longing for more of the dragons. I wanted to know more. I wanted to see more. I just wanted more.

I watched the Bensens, heads pressed together whispering. Mrs. Bensen caught my eye and smiled, the familiar motherly smile I'd come to love. The idea they'd searched for me until they found me, meant I was wanted.

Safely on the ground and in our room for the night, I stood at the glass and linked with Deglan one last time before bed. He came to the window and hovered, pressing his snout against the thick panes. Streaks of steam smudged the window as he breathed. I pressed my hand on the glass feeling the heat through its layers. Something had changed in him, as it had in me, and in the morning, I planned to figure out what that was.

When my head hit the pillow, I fell into a dream immediately. It started like every other, but quickly morphed into something new. I perched on Deglan's back as we raced across the oceans, determination in every rake of his wings.

Two large dragons I'd never seen flew beside us. The smallest was red, and the other was a dark shade of brown. They matched our pace as if they were escorting us to our destination. Deglan didn't seem alarmed.

A large mountain rose in the distance. I knew this was Teken Island and we weren't there to sightsee.

We circled it twice before deciding on a landing place. The next moment, dragons surrounded us. I sat up straight on Deglan's back and watched as a pale green dragon landed feet from where the four of us stood. It hadn't occurred to me to be afraid

I knew this was Lord Edric. The color of his scales matched the tone of his rotting heart.

He snarled at me, signaling the others to do the same. He raised his claws. When it was silent, he called me from Deglan's back, and I listened, still unafraid. He narrowed his eyes, then spat on the ground at my feet.

"You should have died," he said, his voice echoing in my

head.

"But I didn't," I said, lifting my chin in the air, "and now I'm here to dethrone you and appoint a rightful Lord over the Teken."

"By whose authority?" he scoffed.

"By mine," said a voice from behind. A voice I knew at once to be Atticus.

Chapter Seventeen
DEGLAN · THE DRAGON

The dream Meia and I shared, pinged in my head the entire morning. It woke me earlier than I'd intended to be up, but the details rattled me. I didn't know Atticus, but the name belonging to the voice held authority. Authority Lord Edric would be forced to listen to.

But who was he? Would Meia know?

The early morning twilight made it easier for me to find her window again, and I tapped until Mr. Bensen's figure appeared in the waning night.

Who's Atticus? I asked him through the thick glass.

He frowned. *We'll meet you in the forest behind the hotel. Stay hidden.*

Once we were together again, I watched the Bensen's reactions as I retold my dream, wondering if they could decipher its meaning. At the mention of the name Atticus, Meia shot to her feet.

"I had the same dream! Atticus is the guy I emailed who found your dragon island."

"He found it? When?" I tilted my head trying to make sense of her words.

Meia dug through her backpack and offered crumpled pages to Mr. Bensen's outstretched hand. "He said he had removed the page over ten years ago, and wasn't sure how I had pulled up the information. He found Teken Island by accident when he was exploring the Cook Islands, but he said, 'You can't help them.' And told me to stay away."

Mr. Bensen looked between Meia and the pages. His brows knit together when he turned to Mrs. Bensen, whose face was pale as a ghost and her eyes as round as the full moon.

"Grace, it could be a complete coincidence," Mr. Bensen said in a reassuring tone.

She shook her head jubilantly. "No, Gabriel. It makes sense. It makes perfect sense."

"What does?" Meia's confused question sounded more like a plea.

"Atticus..." Mr. Bensen began then stopped. I could tell he was unsure of what he should say. He rubbed the back of his neck and looked to his wife for help.

"Atticus... is your father's name, Meia." When the words left Mrs. Bensen's lips, Meia turned white. "When your parents were attacked, we were there."

I stared at Mrs. Bensen, unable to believe what she claimed. How could she have been there? She would have to be...

Large tears rolled down Meia's cheeks as Mr. Bensen knelt beside her.

"It's true," he said, face-to-face with Meia. "We found your boat. The Tekens had already attacked and left you for dead. We tried to save your mother."

"We did everything we could, Meia," Mrs. Bensen turned to me. "Everything." She joined Mr. Bensen on the ground in front of Meia. "It was too late. She was already gone. Your father, Atticus, still clung weakly to life. He would have died if we hadn't..." She looked up at me again. "You see, Meia, when a human receives even a drop of dragon blood in their veins, legend says they too will transform into a dragon. It was our only hope of saving your father."

Meia's eyes widened, "How did you...?"

"You're dragons," I said, unable to hide my grin. "You're Zamen Dragons."

"What?" Meia stepped away from the Bensens, her eyes searching their faces in disbelief. "How can they be dragons? They look like humans!" The hysteria burst out with her words.

"Zamens are shifters. They can switch between human and dragon anytime they want with no lingering effects."

The Bensens didn't have to say a word. The smiles on their faces as I spoke said everything.

"Does that mean Meia's father's a Zamen?" I couldn't hold back the excitement bubbling through my veins.

"Hold on, Deglan. It's possible that it isn't the same Atticus. We don't even know if he lived or if the transformation was complete."

"But it's possible?" Meia asked, color returning to her face.

"It's not only possible, Meia, it's probable," I said, beaming with pride. "Dragon blood is powerful, and the stories say it heals even the most broken man."

Meia's eyes filled with hope.

"Whoa, whoa, wait a minute." Mr. Bensen held up his hands. "We have to find Atticus to confirm he's even alive," he said, patting down the energy in the air.

"He's alive! He emailed me!" Energy burst from Meia's words. "My father is alive!"

Chapter Eighteen
MEIA - THE HUMAN

Mr. and Mrs. Bensen checked out of the hotel while I waited with Deglan in the forest. It felt so natural to be with him, the whole world suddenly made sense. *No wonder I dreamed of dragons; my father was one.*

I giggled to myself thinking that I'd been living with dragons for the past three months and never knew it. Cate would freak when she found out.

We boarded a plane to Australia with Deglan catching our tailwind. Near the end of the flight, Mrs. Bensen excused herself for the bathroom and as I watched her go I caught Mr. Bensen peering at me over his magazine.

"Can I ask you a question?" I said, poking my finger at the monitor nestled in the seatback. "What happened the night you found us? I mean, why did you leave Atticus on Zamen Island?"

Mr. Bensen raised an eyebrow and set his magazine in his lap, "He was in bad shape and needed special care as his body healed. We knew he would receive it with the Zamens, so it was an obvious choice."

"And, what about me? How come you didn't just keep me?"

Mr. Bensen grasped my hand between his own. "Meia, we've never had any hatchlings of our own so we knew nothing about raising anything, let alone a human. We'd debated on just winging it, but in the end, we thought you'd be better off with your own kind."

"I guess you probably didn't have formula or anything, huh?"

He laughed and put his arm around me. "Nope, definitely no formula on Zamen Island. But, you know, once we left you, it was all we could do to not wonder if we'd made the right decision. After a few months, we had to accept it and move on."

"What made you change your mind?"

"Grace and I both tried to hide our doubts from each other until one day we just agreed we'd done the wrong thing. We read every baby book published while we searched for you, but the foster care system in California is pretty confidential. The weeks turned into months, the months turned into years. But we continued to search, certain you belonged with the dragons."

"And you just happened to be around when I lost my last placement?" I puckered my lips, holding in the groan that wanted to escape when I remembered the fateful day I'd been slotted for a new home. It hadn't been my fault. I couldn't control the nightmares the other children in the house were having. But after the youngest said she saw dragons outside her window, I had to go. "Wait a minute," I said, pulling back from his embrace. "You didn't by chance peek into Mr. and Mrs. Roland's windows while I was there, did you?"

Mr. Bensen's eyes went round and he bit the side of his lip. "Maybe once or twice."

"Ha!" I said, pointing at him. "It was you! It wasn't my fault after all!" I sagged into the seat and released a loud sigh of relief.

Mr. Bensen laughed. "No, it wasn't you. We'd been trying to find a way for you to get out of that one. They didn't seem all that interested in you."

"Nah, they were okay." I stuck my feet on the armrests in front of me. "But how did you know it was me? I mean, years later, I'm sure I didn't look the same."

Mr. Bensen tapped my knee, signaling me to put my feet down. "No, you certainly didn't look the same. You'd grown a few inches, had a few more freckles," he said, poking my cheek. "But the Dragon's Promise on the back of your neck confirmed it."

My hand wandered up to my neck, feeling for raised skin, or any sign of the mark.

"You won't be able to feel it, or see it. And for that matter, most dragon's can't either. You have to know what you are looking for."

"What does it look like?" I craned my neck, twisting my eyes trying to see what I imagined as rays of sunshine shooting from my neck.

"They all look different, but yours looks like a little shield."

I watched Mr. Bensen's eyes as they roamed over my face, wondering if I should voice the next question on my tongue. "Mr. Bensen, what happens if we do find my dad?"

Mr. Bensen's eyes softened. "What do you mean?"

"With you and Mrs. Bensen? You guys have been great... but..." I didn't know how to say what was on my mind. While I was worried about hurting them, it was my dad.

"Oh Meia," Mr. Bensen said. "We knew this day could come. We care for you very much but our goal has always been to reunite you with your father if possible." He patted my hand, his smile reaching his eyes.

"What are you two talking about?" Mrs. Bensen asked, buckling herself into the seat again.

Mr. Bensen winked at me and flipped open his magazine, "Oh you know, the weather."

"Ha," she said, grabbing the magazine from his grasp. "I don't believe you."

I watched as my foster parents playfully bantered back and forth. Any child would be lucky to have such a foster placement. Mr. Bensen flashed me a knowing smile when he'd retrieved his magazine and a warm fuzzy feeling circled in my belly. If we couldn't find my dad, maybe they would adopt me.

My heart quickened when the wheels of the plane touched down. Outside the cabin walls was a new adventure, one that may lead me to my dragon father.

We met Deglan in the Australian outback under the cover of night. Kangaroos hopped nearby, while wallabies hung out in the trees, seemingly unfazed by Deglan's appearance. The Bensens transformed behind the trees, but when they came into view, I was in awe.

A tall, brown dragon lumbered toward us, his regal scales shimmering in the moonlight. I could tell this was Mr. Bensen by the way his head cocked to the side as he eyed me. Though he was huge, Deglan still dwarfed him. The red dragon to his left was much more petite and proper, definitely Mrs. Bensen. Her horns were more like the curly locks of her human hair that rippled down her back. It was curious how much they mirrored their human forms.

"Meia, you'll ride Deglan," Mr. Bensen said with a bob of his large dragon head. It was strange hearing his voice come from a dragon snout, but it somehow fit perfectly. "Deglan, if we run into trouble, I need you to obey without question."

"Yes, sir," Deglan said then laid himself down in the dirt to allow me to climb on his back.

Mrs. Bensen used Deglan's leather pack to fasten a makeshift saddle to him. Fortunately, it had a seatbelt of sorts to keep me securely strapped to his back. I'd seen how fast Deglan could travel and falling off at any speed, let alone that one, would make for a rough landing.

"Are we all ready?"

I nodded, unsure if I would ever be ready to fly on the back of a dragon. Sure, I'd dreamed about it all my life, but tied behind the massive blue wings on either side of me, I had second thoughts. I closed my eyes, leaned forward, and gripped the leather straps in front of me.

With a few erratic movements, the wind rushed on every side and the echo of wings bounced through the air. The sheer weightlessness made my stomach do flip-flops as the air currents pressed against my face. I waited a good minute before I convinced myself I was acting like a baby and opened my eyes.

To say I gasped would be the understatement of the century. I think it was more like a gasp, squeal, and a hip-hip-hooray all in one syllable.

It was awesome!

We flew at the same level as the clouds on the horizon. The remainder of the sunset drowned in the ocean beside me. Deglan's head slithered through the jet streams, his body following in fluid motion. It was graceful and exactly the way I dreamed it would be.

The Bensens flew just ahead, on an even path toward the unknown. The unknown, that could very well be my father.

Chapter Nineteen
DEGLAN · THE DRAGON

Meia fit perfectly upon the saddle Mrs. Bensen had fashioned. It was like she'd been made to ride only me. When her hands touched my scales, a current flowed through them, energizing my every movement. The prospect of finding her father caused nervous ripples to flow through every vein of her body.

If the dream were true, we would find Atticus, go to Teken Island, and confront Lord Edric, something I did not look forward to. But then what? Would Atticus really have the authority to overthrow Edric and appoint a new Lord? And what in heaven's name did all this have to do with Meia, me, or my mark?

My head swelled with all the questions and thoughts. Meia patted my neck and brought my attention back to the task at hand. The Bensens swooped down through the murky abyss. Dew clung to my wings as we followed and hovered just under the cloud cover. After hours of travel with nothing but blue foamy water below us, an island rose in the distance, radiating the Zamen energy cloak. Dragons could see through this cloak, but until you were inside its barriers, humans could not.

We circled the island and landed on a hilltop near the western slopes that were covered in a extraordinary shade of green. The moon poked through the clouds, casting small patches of light sporadically onto the grass.

Mr. Bensen warned us to remain silent when we arrived. Our two clans were rivals, and although neither made a practice of attacking hatchlings or adolescents, Mr. Bensen said my size would lead them to believe that I was a full-grown dragon and something to fear. It was strange to think that adults would consider me a threat, but I towered over the Bensens, which meant I would dwarf others as well.

"Why do you trespass on this land?" A voice echoed through the night.

I twisted my head in every direction, looking for the voice, ready to take flight at the first sign of attack.

"We didn't mean to trespass," Mr. Bensen called. "I'm Gabriel Bensen, Zamen dragon, returning to Zamen Island with friends. I thought this was Sterling's land."

A small growl rippled through the nearby bushes and a chill scurried up my spine like a mouse running from an owl. A series of sniffs sliced the dewy air. An animal jumped from the bushes and landed in front of me, baring its large, jagged, white teeth. I recoiled, prepared to jump into the sky.

"Wait!" Mr. Bensen said, stretching his arm in front of me. "He's a friend and only a hatchling."

The animal sniffed at the air. In the moonlight, it looked like a large cat with saliva dripping from its fangs. He narrowed his eyes on me, then snorted.

"Gabriel Bensen, it's been many years since you've been on Zamen land. Your status isn't clear."

"I know. It's been a long time, but I need to find Sterling."

He glowered at Mr. Bensen now. A low, guttural rumble reverberated from his pursed lips.

"Who's there?" A voice carried through the night from somewhere down the hill.

Without another word, the animal bounded through the bushes and down the opposite side of the hill. The trees swayed under the pressure of whatever came next.

"Steady, Deglan," Mr. Bensen said, his arm still outstretched to me.

"Gabriel?" The friendly voice carried through the trees. "Gabriel, is that you?" The face of a dark green dragon appeared through the foliage, a bright smile on his scaly face. "Gabriel! As I live and breathe!" The dragon roared forward and grasped Mr. Bensen in a friendly squeeze.

"Sterling, my friend," Mr. Bensen laughed, embracing the dragon.

"Grace, dear, you don't look a day older," Sterling said in his thick British accent. "What brings you two back to Zamen?"

Mr. Bensen pointed at Meia and me. The green dragon turned and froze in his tracks. "Oh? Is this...?"

"Sterling, this is Deglan; he's a Teken *hatchling*."

Sterling bobbed his head in amusement. He looked me over, sizing me up. His eyes rested on my forearm and I felt it tingle. He shrugged, then looked at Meia, who still sat terrified on my back.

"And you my dear?" said the cordial, elder-dragon.

"This is the child...," Mrs. Bensen said. "Meia." Her eyes drifted from Meia to Sterling, who immediately registered understanding.

He clasped his paws together and exclaimed, "By the dragon's fire! So good to have you all! Come, come, let's go have some cider and discuss your business." Sterling hurried away before anyone could say another word. Mrs. Bensen followed the elder-dragon.

"Come on you two," Mr. Bensen said, pushing his way through the bushes after the others.

"Are you okay up there?" I sensed her uneasiness.

"Something doesn't feel right," she said in a barely audible whisper. "What was that thing?"

"I'm not sure," I said, eyeing the bushes where the creature had vanished. A lump rose in my throat when I saw a pair of red eyes glaring at me.

"Deglan?" Mr. Bensen's voice startled me. He stepped back into the clearing and waved for us.

I twisted my head towards the trees but the eyes were gone.

"Coming." I lumbered toward safety, the eyes burned in my memory. The haze of danger choked the air as a warning... this wasn't the last time we would see those eyes.

Chapter Twenty
MEIA - THE HUMAN

"I'm so sorry my door isn't big enough for you, Sir Deglan," Sterling said, now in human form. He was a great deal older than Mr. Bensen and looked a bit like one of Einstein's relatives with his gray hair spurting in all directions. "I have never had the opportunity to prepare for..." He stopped mid-thought and bobbed his head back and forth. He laughed at himself then poked at the large kettle on the fire in front of us.

Sterling was weird. In dragon form, he was as acceptable as any human could feel about a dragon, but as a human, he made my skin crawl in ripples. I couldn't decide if it was because he seemed a step ahead of everything we said or if he was just an odd grandfather type. I wished he hadn't sent the Bensens away to gather Atticus, who was indeed still on the island. They'd told me to trust Sterling and to listen to what he said, but that didn't make him any less weird.

Sterling ladled the concoction from the kettle into large mugs that looked like Barbie furniture in Deglan's paws. The steaming, golden liquid in my cup smelled of both spices and fruit.

"Its cider," Sterling said, taking a long drink of his own. "The best apples in all of Zamen were sacrificed to make that for you. Drink up."

I eyed the liquid, then looked up at Deglan who was no doubt wondering how to drink from the small mug with his massive lips.

Sterling laughed with contagious repercussions, which eased some of the nervous tension. "So sorry, Deglan. Why don't you take the kettle instead of that small thing?"

Deglan didn't hesitate, but took the pot from the fire and sipped from its black rim. "It's the best I've ever tasted." The smile on Deglan's face made the remainder of my anxiety melt away.

I sipped slowly, waiting for something profound. I half thought it was a magic potion intended to make something happen that shouldn't. I smacked my lips together and smiled. It tasted like an explosion of apples in my mouth. I took another sip, and as the warm, brown liquid rolled down my throat, a sense of serenity passed over me. Maybe it *was* a magic potion.

"Very well then," Sterling said, setting his empty mug on the log beside him. "Let's get on with it. It may surprise you to realize I know a great deal more than you think I do. Gabriel was wise to come to me. We need to discuss important matters before they get back with Atticus."

My heart thudded in my chest. "Important matters?"

"Oh, yes, no doubt you have discovered you're different," he said with a twinkle in his eye. He turned to Deglan. "...and you, Deglan, can't ignore your mammoth size and dragon mark, eh?" He motioned with his hand and wobbled back and forth on his rear. "You know you're connected, but have no idea why." He grinned, pleased with himself.

"How do you know anything about me? I'm a human girl," I said, wondering if he was some sort of magician or something.

"I'm a Marvel."

"A what?"

"A Marvel," he said, standing. The fire rose when he did. "You know, I see things others can't, know things I shouldn't, and sometimes I can even see parts of the future." He wagged his eyebrows at me, which reminded me of caterpillars doing the tango.

I cocked my head sideways and gave him the 'Are you serious?' look I should be famous for.

He gave me the 'I'm very serious' look as he stoked the

fire. "Meia, Atticus is indeed your father and he does know of you."

Cider sputtered from my lips. The warm liquid slid down my throat unwelcomed, making me choke. Questions immediately pounded my head about why he'd never come to find me.

Deglan tried to comfort me with a nudge.

I was sure he could feel or even hear all the questions that fired like a combat machine gun.

"Don't judge too quickly, Meia. He only learned about you recently but before we can discuss that, I have other news you need to hear."

My heart fluttered in my chest.

"First, you must know I've had visions of you both since you were born. Both you and Deglan were born on the same day, to those whose friendship was forbidden."

"Why are dragons forbidden to associate with humans?" The likely answer to my question was dragons might eat the humans. But somehow, I knew it was more than that.

"Legend says that humans were the downfall of dragons. Dragons once populated the whole earth, much like the humans do now. They called most of our clan species dino-bots or something."

"Dinosaurs?" I corrected. "You mean all the dinosaurs were different clans of dragons?"

"Oh yes, there we go. Dinosaurs. I try to ignore the folly when I hear it. All but two clans — the Tekens and the Zamens — were wiped out. It took nearly a century to get enough dragon hatchlings to begin to repopulate the culture. We lived in harmony once," he said, nodding his head.

Deglan frowned. "I find that difficult to believe."

"I would bet you do. You've grown up only knowing them as a rival. Dragons are a pretty stubborn species," Sterling said, winking at me. "They separated the clans to stop the fighting. Each clan believes they are the stronger, better clan. They've been building their ranks in hope of taking over the earth again."

Deglan choked on what remained of his cider, his words coming out in raspy breaths. "The dragons want to take over the earth again?"

"Well, some still do. This is why the alliance was formed."

"The what?" I crinkled my face in question.

"The alliance between the dragons and the humans. More rightly so, the Teken dragons. When the Bensens rescued you and your father from the boat, another alliance was formed — one between the Zamens and the humans."

"So there are two alliances with the humans?"

His eyes twinkled again. "No, there is but one. Meia, you have a scar on your ankle, yes?"

"Yeah," I said, tugging on my jeans. *How did he know about my scar?*

"That's from Deglan."

"What?" I pulled up my pant leg. The scar gleamed white in the firelight.

"Yes. Purely by accident, but it's from him. With that mark, he gave you some of his own DNA molecules, binding the alliance between the Teken people and you, a human. He didn't give you enough DNA to change into a full dragon, but enough to give you traits and the ability to enable the link between your minds."

Deglan and I stared into each other's eyes in awe of this news. The connection was real. I wasn't just a silly girl daydreaming. I was part dragon.

Chapter Twenty - One
DEGLAN - THE DRAGON

"Do you mean... Meia is part dragon?" I couldn't pull my eyes away from her. Now that I thought about it, her hazel green eyes did have a few familiar flecks I'd seen in dragons before, and her brows and eyes were vaguely slanted, reminiscent of a dragon.

"Yes, she's part dragon, but a very small part," Sterling said. I heard the smile in his voice. "However, with her birth, your birth, and the DNA transfer... legend became a reality and Lord Edric knew it."

"Legend? Which legend? I'm only aware of the one about my mark." When he didn't speak right away, I forced myself to look at Sterling.

His eyes jumped around in the firelight, the smile on his face no longer visible. "Lord Edric had no idea your mark would become what it is." He pointed at my forearm. "He sensed something different about you the day he saw your mark, but he had no idea you would be the one."

"The one of what?" Meia spoke up.

"Legend said one would come and unify the clans, one whose connection to all the clans was obvious... and who bears the ancient mark of the dragon.

The firelight danced off my dragon mark, making it glow as it had in the dim torchlight of my room back on Teken Island.

"He's only ten," Meia said, breaking the awkward silence.

"Only ten?" The shock registered across Sterling's face as he peered at her. "Can not a tenth year do marvelous things in the human world? Ten is the age of everything as a dragon. Ten is when a dragon rises to become who he is."

His hands flew into the air and his eyes bore into mine. "It's no mistake that they make the Rising Ceremony on the tenth year, Deglan Borian. Ten is an important year of growth and understanding." He turned to Meia again, frowning and rubbing his elongated chin. "To say he's only ten is like saying there's only one way from here to there. It's foolishness. It means nothing." He plopped back into his seat.

Meia and I stared at him, confused at why he'd had such an outburst.

"Why me?" I didn't want to say, I'm only ten, but that was all I could think now. Surely, there was another more qualified dragon to do this job. Surely, there was another with a mark like a dragon.

"Deglan, you're the only one with the mark *and* the only one with a connection to both the clans. It *will* be you. You may not understand or accept it now, but it's how it must be."

"Okay, then that should be easy enough. We can just call a truce between the two clans."

Sterling shook his head, his face heavy with remorse. "Lord Edric will do anything in his power to see that this legend never comes to reality. Even kill." The regret in his eyes told me what he said was true. My mom had written about it in her journal, which meant it had already begun when I was born. He *would* do anything.

"In my dream, Atticus was the one who had the authority to dethrone Lord Edric," I said, meeting his expectant eyes.

"You've dreamed about this day?"

"So have I," added Meia. "We dreamed it on the same night."

Meia and I took turns telling Sterling the details of the dream, his eyes intent on each of our faces as we spoke. When we fell silent, he tapped his chin methodically, his eyes bobbing back and forth, his head tilting from one side to the other as he deliberated.

"I think your dream has signified three things. First,

you're indeed the one," he said, pointing a pudgy finger in my direction. "Second, you, Meia, and Atticus have to be together to dethrone him."

Meia groaned.

"Third, Atticus will give the authority to you, Deglan, because you're the only one of the trinity alliance born with full dragon blood. You hold pieces of each of the three within your own blood, for you have Meia's DNA in you as well. Atticus is Meia's father and now a Zamen dragon. Your mother is also Zamen, Deglan."

My head popped up. "She is?"

"Yes, but it's been hidden from the Teken for fear they would cast her away."

I grinned knowing this made me a half-blood.

"Deglan, with you being half Teken, half Zamen, and a wee bit human... you became the one."

I clicked my tongue, thinking about his last words. "I wasn't born the *one*?"

Sterling shook his head. "Your mark was like every other's when you were born. Probably a star or crescent moon, like the rest of the clans, but the moment you received a part of Meia, your mark changed and has been growing inside you until this day."

"So, had Meia not come to Teken Island, I might have never become the *one*?"

"Correct. Don't get me wrong Deglan, this legend was meant to be fulfilled by you, no one else. Lords before you have been doing everything to stop it. The clans have gotten tired of the lords ruling them with an iron fist. They want unity and you will bring it, even if Lord Edric doesn't welcome it."

"So..." I struggled with what he was telling me. "That means I have to be the one to dethrone Edric?" My stomach churned uneasily.

"Yes, only you have the perfect triangular blood alliance. Once Lord Edric sees the mark, the girl, and the Zamen Dragon that is Atticus, he will know he has lost."

"He won't just give up without a fight..." Meia's small voice echoed beside me. "Will he?"

"Unfortunately, no... he won't."

"Well, that sucks," Meia said. She looked so serious as she said it, but something in me broke after the words rolled off her tongue.

I erupted into laughter, which made her laugh, then Sterling joined in.

"I wish I knew the joke," the familiar voice came from behind me. I turned my head and saw a dark-haired human standing beside Gabriel and Grace Bensen. The human from my dream.

Atticus.

Chapter Twenty - Two
MEIA - THE HUMAN

His voice echoed in my head, and I knew at once who it was, but I couldn't bring myself to turn for fear he would disappear.

Please, God, don't let this be a dream. Please don't take him away again.

Sterling gave me an encouraging nod when I stood to my feet. My heart pounded so hard it felt like it wanted out of my chest. I held my eyes to the ground as I walked around Deglan, willing myself to look up. I didn't want to see the disappointment on his face when he saw whom I'd become. I wasn't as pretty as Patricia Tison; she'd told me so many times in the schoolyard. I didn't have long, sleek hair like Cate or sparkling blue eyes like Ms. Keller or red curls like Mrs. Bensen. Nothing stood out about my flat medium-length brown hair, freckles dotting my pudgy nose, and hazel-green eyes.

I knew I would have to look up and meet his gaze, but I was so afraid. Everyone remained silent, but I was unable to move even an eyelash. Deglan nudged my back in encouragement and, when he touched me, a surge of calm rushed through my body.

"Meia?" the breathless voice called out.

I couldn't tell if he was disappointed, but I knew it was time. I closed my eyes and tilted my chin up, convincing myself that regardless of what he thought, I liked who I was, and I was silly worrying about what he thought of me. I filled my lungs with the warm night air, then opened my eyes.

A man knelt between Mr. and Mrs. Bensen, his disheveled black hair in a mass on his head and his hands were over his mouth. My eyes met his and I saw the tears collecting at their crinkly corners.

"Daddy?" My voice cracked and I took off in a run toward his now open arms.

The moment we touched, I felt energy rush through my body and immediately knew he was proud to be my father. I felt the tears on his cheeks as they pressed against mine.

Atticus was my father.

I'm not sure how long I remained in his embrace before he picked me up and joined the others by the fireside. I rested my head on his shoulder, unwilling to let him go. I thought if I let him go, he would be lost forever.

Would this mean I could live on Zamen Island with him? The questions pounded my head as I listened to them talk.

"Deglan," Mr. Bensen said from somewhere beside me. "How are you doing with all this news?"

"I guess, I'm doing as well as one can, after hearing a story like that. Did you know all this when you brought Meia to the Cook Islands?"

"Well, most of it, yes. We weren't sure how much was true and how much was still speculation. Now, the question is, what do we do with all this newfound knowledge?"

I lifted my head from my father's shoulder, but still leaned into him, afraid he would disappear.

"I'm not going anywhere," he whispered and patted my leg. He kissed my hair then joined in the conversation. "If what Sterling says is correct, we have to go to Teken Island and Deglan has to confront Lord Edric at the next lunar eclipse when the whole clan gathers."

"But isn't that only a few weeks away? We can't possibly be ready by then," Mrs. Bensen said.

I looked up at Atticus when he spoke again.

"We have to be ready. The following eclipse isn't for another six months or so."

"What do we have to do to be ready?" Deglan's voice trembled with fear.

I wanted to spring to my feet and rush to him. Instead, I met his eyes and gave a comforting nod. I hoped he understood why I clung to my father.

"We have to teach you how to hunt and fight, Deglan. Edric is not going to give up his throne without a fight."

"His throne? Deglan is going to be the lord?" I stood straight up, pushing out of my father's arms. "He's only ten!" I protested. "How can he be lord over all the Tekens?"

"Meia, he's the one appointed to unify the clans. It's obvious that he should take over as lord of both."

"Do you hear how insane that sounds?" I held my hand up to Sterling, who was no doubt about to protest with his 'ten is grand' speech again. "You can't put a ten-year-old in charge of two clans of dragons. He's not ready, and he won't be ready in two weeks or... or two months... maybe not even two years. How can you expect him to do that?" The firelight danced on the stunned faces. Deglan understood and felt everything I'd said, only I'd gotten to my feet first to say it... well, maybe it was more like I yelled it.

"Meia, it's different for dragons," Mrs. Bensen offered.

"No, it's not," I practically screamed at her. "It's no different. We're both ten. We've both only lived for ten years of life. Maybe in ten more years he might be ready to make life-altering decisions for a whole race of dragons. But right now? Are you serious?" My breath came in short, ragged bursts. I hadn't been this worked up about anything in all my life, but with Deglan's emotions running through my veins, along with the new emotions seeing my father brought to life, I was on fire.

"Meia, you need to calm down," Mr. Bensen said in a firm, but loving, voice.

I sat back beside my father and accepted his warmth around my shoulders again.

"I understand how you feel," Sterling said, speaking directly to Deglan as if he knew those were his feelings as well.

My eyes landed on Deglan and I shook my head in dismay. He looked like a small child afraid of his own shadow, which was difficult to do as an oversized dragon.

The idea that he would be expected to be a warrior, rattled both of us.

"I think we've done enough talking for the night. Let's get some rest and speak again tomorrow," Sterling said, turning toward his dwelling. Before he went in, he turned directly to me. "Sleep well, and I pray you dream tonight." He disappeared into his dwelling and closed the door behind him, leaving us at the fire.

Chapter Twenty - Three
DEGLAN - THE DRAGON

That night I slept tucked around the fire outside Atticus' home. I did dream, but it was the one Meia and I had already shared. Nothing new had shown itself. When I told Sterling the next morning, he seemed confused but dismissed it and went off to take care of his duties.

"Deglan, Mrs. Bensen wants to show me around the island," Meia said, bouncing out the door of the dwelling. "Do you want to come?"

"He can't," Mr. Bensen interrupted. "He has some work to do today."

"Work?" I didn't like the sound of that.

The excitement drained from Meia's face.

"Meia, I'm going to stay behind while you explore with Grace," Atticus said, picking up the leather pack and setting it on a nearby rock. I hadn't seen Atticus in dragon form yet, but I knew he was going to be an impressive sight. Half dragon, half humans were always rumored to be some of the most beautiful dragons that existed. Until yesterday, I thought they were a myth. I silently chuckled, remembering Meia's own words about the mythical dragons. Things can change a lot in a few days.

We watched as Meia and Mrs. Bensen walked down the street and out of sight. When they were well out of earshot, the electricity in the air jolted my senses, making me jump back in alarm.

I watched in awe as Atticus transformed. The air vibrated with power. His head and neck elongated and his hair shifted into spikes protruding from the top of his head and flowing down his back, which rapidly changed into a scaled mass. I assumed the pearl color he emitted would change at any moment, but when he stood in full form, his iridescent white scales gleamed in the sun.

My mind scrambled for an explanation of the white color, but as far as I could recall, Atticus was the only white dragon I'd ever seen.

Mr. Bensen didn't leave time for me to speculate before he ushered us into the sky.

We flew for a few minutes before landing in a nearby field where three other dragons waited — a tall green dragon; a short, stout, black one; and a tan one who looked about as old as any dragon I'd ever seen.

"What are we here for?"

"You must learn to fight," Atticus said, clapping me on the back.

The blood drained from my face as I looked at the other dragons, only now seeing their rugged appearance and scars. They were fighting instructors. "Ummm, what if I don't want to fight?" I said, only loud enough for Atticus to hear.

"Deglan, you need to learn, regardless if you'll need it right away or not."

Mr. Bensen went forward and introduced us. The three instructors looked me over and didn't seem the least bit swayed by my size, though I towered over them by a whole dragon.

Arthus, the old tan dragon, began what would be an hour-long lecture of the logistics of fighting, followed up by the traditions of fair play. Some of the information made the blue of my scales turn green. My stomach churned uneasily; I wasn't sure how I would be able to do some of what they said.

With the lecture over, the black dragon, Naven, demonstrated the basics of fire-breathing. I didn't mean to laugh aloud when he blew his fire across the field, but I knew the "impressive distance" was short of what I'd already seen myself do on the atoll.

Naven narrowed his eyes. "Let's see what you've got, boy."

Atticus and Mr. Bensen nodded me forward and I swallowed hard, hoping whatever I'd done in the forest on Penrhyn could be duplicated on cue. I turned away from the dragons and crouched on all fours. My tail flicked nervously like a cat's, hitting the grass every couple of swings, vibrating the ground. Looking across the field, I judged I had plenty of distance without catching any trees on fire.

I closed my eyes and inhaled so deeply my sides bulged in pain. I released my breath, expecting the fire to erupt over my lips. When it didn't, I took another breath and tried again.

Nothing.

I peered sideways and caught the sarcastic grin of Naven. Heat rose in my veins and I inhaled, this time with fervor and poise. A small growl escaped my parted lips and seemed to light the air afire, shooting an impressive stream of power.

Yes!

I inhaled quickly and blew again, this time the fire burst across the field, catching a dead tree ablaze.

The three instructors began to scream and run in every direction. They looked like a herd of chickens running from the ax. They hurried down to the nearby stream, slurped water, and doused the flames, sending smoke signals into the sky.

I sat up and looked at Atticus and Mr. Bensen who were laughing.

"I guess I passed?"

Chapter Twenty - Four
MEIA - THE HUMAN

It was an odd feeling to walk down the streets of Zamen Island and see the dragons mingling with those in human form. I might have dreamed about dragons all my life, but there were never other humans in my dream.

I was amazed at how closely their houses resembled Dutch villages I'd seen in my history books. The large, brightly painted shutters on the windows dwarfed the actual houses. Thatched wood decorated the walls in odd places, vines grew up their weaves, and flowers bloomed from odd places. My feet fell upon the uneven cobbled streets, the colored rocks of every shape and size making it difficult for me to walk in a straight path. A dragon pulled a cart in front of us, the clickity-clack of the wheels, rolling over the uneven surface.

"Grace Bensen?" A voice beckoned from beside us.

We turned to see a woman with short, wavy, dark hair, waving her arm at us. The woman jumped from the log she'd been sitting on and hurried toward her gate, pushing her way onto the street.

"Theresa!" Mrs. Bensen rushed to the waiting embrace.

"As I live and breathe. What brings you back to Zamen?" She turned quickly to me and barely caught her breath before continuing. "What a beautiful hatchling you have. She has curious color eyes. I've only seen that one other time in all my years." She grasped my face and turned it from side to side. "Wow, what is that on the back of her—"

"Ah, Theresa, always the most observant. This is my foster daughter, Meia. She isn't a Zamen." Mrs. Bensen gripped my shoulder and pulled me affectionately toward her. "She's from California."

She didn't say it, but I knew Mrs. Bensen was trying to tell Theresa I was human.

"Oh? California?" She squinted and her left eyebrow rose in question. "California. Yes, okay. Well, dear, I would love to say it was nice to see you again." And without another word she pressed through her gate, entered her house, and shut the door.

Mrs. Bensen stared after her in shock. "I'm sorry, Meia. The dragons..."

"It's okay, Mrs. Bensen. Deglan told me a little about why dragons don't like us."

She escorted me down the lane, arm still on my shoulder. "Oh, he did? What did he say?"

"That humans were the reason you went into hiding to preserve the race."

"Are they still teaching that in instruction? What a bunch of hooey," she said and waved her hand as if swatting a fly.

"Humans aren't the reason the dragons went into hiding?"

"Nope. Humans and dragons once lived together in harmony, each laboring for one another, similar to how farming communities work. Dragons hunted and kept the borders secure. Humans grew the crops and took care of our sick. It was a fabulous society to be part of."

"You talk like you've lived it."

"I have," she said, with a wide smile.

"How long ago was this?" Surely, Mrs. Bensen can't be that old.

"It was long ago, longer than I care to admit."

I searched Mrs. Bensen's face. Fine lines peeked from the corners of her eyes and a few more dotted her forehead. "Are we talking a hundred years or more?"

She bobbed her head back and forth, unwilling to give me a number.

"How long can dragons live?" I asked, thinking I could get a time frame for reference.

She pinched her lips, similar to how Ms. Keller did when she was figuring out how to deal with me. "Eight hundred years, give or take a few hundred."

I stopped midstride and looked up in astonishment.

"Don't look at me like that; I didn't say *I* was that old."

"How do they live so long?"

Mrs. Bensen led me forward again. "I don't really know."

The wheels in my head twisted and clicked at an alarming pace. I opened my mouth before I could think. "Then someone is pretty stupid for thinking Deglan is the one to take over."

"Meia." Her eyebrows shot together in admonishment.

"I'm serious. Dragons live to be a thousand years old, yet a ten-year-old is supposed to somehow rule over them? Does anyone realize how crazy that sounds? Or is it *really* just me?"

She looked off into the distance, thinking about the words I'd spoken. "I know it sounds odd, Meia. But the ways of a dragon are different from that of a human. Legend is seldom ignored, especially when one comes to pass."

"Regardless, I think someone needs to rethink this whole idea. No one in their right mind would put a ten-year-old in charge of a whole country. No dragon should either."

"Unfortunately, it's not up to you Meia. It's not even up to Deglan. It's just what will happen."

I groaned and kicked a loose stone in the path. It shot from my foot and hit the backside of someone leaning over a woodpile. I covered my mouth, "Oops."

"Hey! What's the deal?" The Zamen roared, turning to face us.

"Sorry about that. My..." Mrs. Bensen hesitated long enough that it was awkward for her to continue.

"It was an accident," I said.

The dragon narrowed his eyes. "What's she doing here?"

"I'm sorry?" Mrs. Bensen asked, even though I was quite sure she knew what he was asking.

"The human. Why's she here? By whose authority was she allowed on this island?" His voice raised to a loud roar and anger radiated from every word he spoke.

I stepped back, and hit something sturdy. When I turned, I my heart sank into my toes. Another large dragon stood right behind me, his menacing eyes peering down at us. I grabbed at Mrs. Bensen, but was shocked to feel a scaly body under my fingertips. I jumped back from the touch before I realized she was a dragon now.

"Get on," she commanded and I wasted no time in following her orders.

The dragons in the street increased in number by the moment, seemingly hearing the growl as a call for help. As each circled, growls rolled over their lips and echoed off the walls of the nearby houses.

"Grab hold," Mrs. Bensen said, ready to leap from the ground and out of any harm's way.

"To what?" I screeched back. I laid my body against her back, grasped at her sides, and prepared for the launch into the sky.

"STOP!" A voice echoed and silenced the crowd. I swiveled my head and saw Sterling, in dragon form, padding quickly down the tapered corridor. "What in blazes is going on here?"

The dragons backed up to allow Sterling access.

"This Zamen has brought a human among us," spat the first dragon. The crowed hissed in disapproval, growls again moving through the ranks.

"Is there a problem with a human being in your midst?" Sterling asked, turning to the crowd. "Do you still believe the tales of old? That they are here to steal, kill, and destroy? That is dragonwash!" He paced the circle, glaring into the faces of our opposers. "This human is here on my bidding," he said.

Every dragon in the crowd voiced their disbelief, the chaos bouncing in my ears like ping pong balls.

"Yes. If you want to blame someone, blame me." His

voice rose with his anger. "Blame me for wanting the Zamen Clan to be more than what we've become. Blame me for wanting a better life for the dragons. Blame me for wanting unity among the clans." He whirled abruptly to his right. "Godfrey, when was the last time you saw your mother?"

The gray dragon he addressed put his head down. "Not for over a hundred years, sir."

"Matthew," he spoke to the dragon on his left. "When was the last time any of your hatchmates were together?"

The tan dragon backed up slowly, but didn't answer.

"Which of you is pure blood? Come forward so I can let you speak and have your say." He looked at the crowd waiting for someone to step out. "That's what I thought. Not one of you has the right to judge this child. She will bring hope back to all dragons. Not only the Zamens. Her presence means unification is on the horizon."

Gasps of disbelief washed over the crowd.

"You'll see your mother again and you'll see your hatchmates." He then turned to the large dragon that had started the uproar. His voice was calm and he put a claw on his shoulder. "And you Jemes, you will see your wife and hatchlings again."

The anger in Jemes' face melted away as he looked up.

"Do you want to be reunited with your loved ones? Then believe me and in the legend that speaks of this day. By the dragon's claw, it *will be* reality."

The crowd erupted in cheers as I slid down Mrs. Bensen's back. When I turned, she had taken human form again.

"Climb on, you two," Sterling said, motioning. He bid the crowd farewell and lifted into the sky. "Grace," he spoke gruffly, as we soared through the air. "Teach this girl to fight. You were lucky this time."

The thought of fighting a dragon made my stomach twist into knots. I couldn't fight dragons... or could I?

Chapter Twenty - Five
DEGLAN - THE DRAGON

The three instructors stood in front of me, their black faces singed. Two weren't smiling. The third, Arthus, the very old tan dragon, had one eye closed and the other trained on the trees in the distance. He was probably wondering if they would burst into flames again.

Naven tried to blame the length of my fire-breathing on the wind, but I could tell by the way he spoke he didn't believe it himself.

Henry, the green dragon, cleared his throat and gave me a dismissive smile. "Well, Deglan," he said in a pinched, cackly voice.

I glanced over at Mr. Bensen and Atticus, who shook their heads, reminding me not to burst into laughter again.

"We're going to see how well you do with hunting. Surely, you've hunted before?" The way he raised his brows told me he knew Tekens weren't allowed to hunt unless it was their job.

I shook my head and watched his expression twist into triumph. I had a feeling he was going to make this extremely difficult.

He wrung his claws together and looked to Naven, whose lopsided mischievous grin made goose bumps break out over my body. Henry was about to begin what I assumed was a lengthy explanation of hunting and why it was important to fighting tactics, when a small dragon, no bigger than a dog scampered into the clearing.

"Sirs, you're needed on the hill," he said, looking nervously among us.

"We are in the middle of—"

"It's back," the dragon said. "You're needed posthaste."

Henry cursed under his breath. "You'll have to teach him, Arthus." He jostled the old dragon beside him, seemingly waking him from slumber, then pushed off into the sky, followed closely by Naven.

We looked to Arthus, who stood slumped over, pondering his command. His one eye was still closed, but at least he looked at me.

"Well, I'm not sure what he was expecting me to teach you. I haven't hunted in years."

Everyone laughed.

"Gabriel and I can teach him. Why don't you go get cleaned up?" Atticus said. He gestured at the sulfur from the tree fire still covering the tan dragon's face.

The elder-dragon wiped his cheek and opened both eyes to peer at his claw. "Where'd that come from? Hmm, yes. I will go clean up. Good day, sirs."

Mr. Bensen pinched his lips together then coughed to cover his chuckle. "Okay, then. Let's start with something easy."

On cue, a rabbit jumped into the clearing and froze.

"Catch it, Deglan."

"Wha...? You mean like, just chase right after it?"

The two dragons nodded.

"You'd better get moving. He looks as if he's about to dart."

Sure enough, the rabbit took off across the field.

"Don't kill it. Just catch and release it."

I rolled my eyes and took off toward the rabbit disappearing into the brush. I groaned as a branch smacked me in the face, sending me reeling backward into the field.

Atticus gave me an encouraging nod.

It took a while for me to finally catch the darn thing. Rabbits are fast and don't care if they run you face first into the trunk of a tree (or two) trying to get away. Nevertheless, on the fortieth try, my reflexes kicked in. I darted from the trees and blocked every move the rabbit made. The work was tiresome, but I felt my senses heightening. I could hear his feet on the damp ground and when I sensed the motion in his ears, I could tell which way he would dart. I caught the rabbit at least ten times before it lay limp in defeat, exhausted from being chased by an oversized dragon.

Atticus and Mr. Bensen clapped in approval when I returned to their side.

"So I did okay, Mr. Bensen?"

"Please, Deglan, call me Gabriel. And yes, you did excellent. I've never seen another dragon pick up on the senses as you have."

We took long drinks from the nearby stream. I'd thought my training was complete for the day until Atticus stood to his feet and watched an albatross dart across the sky.

"Now it's time for the real challenge," Atticus said, wagging his eyebrows, then jumping into the sky.

Gabriel and I followed him up and over the clouds, rising high in the afternoon winds. It was odd to be flying during the daytime hours, something I hadn't done much of yet. A strange tingle raced across my scales and I felt as if the whole island watched me. I pushed the thoughts aside, when I could see no one on the ground gawking at us. Was it even possible that all the Zamens knew of the legend? Even if they did, I convinced myself they wouldn't realize it was coming to pass before their eyes. To them, I was just a tenth year taking a flight with two elders.

"Time to catch a bird, Deglan," Atticus said.

"What? Up here? Now?" I looked sideways at Gabriel to see if Atticus was serious or not. Hunting on the ground was one thing; hunting in the air sent a whole new shockwave of panic through my scales. Sure, I could hit a tree and bounce back, but plummeting out of the sky at crazy speeds toward the ground, didn't sound like my idea of a good time... or something I could easily recover from.

"Yes, now. There are albatross all over these parts. Pick one and go for it."

"You can do it, Deglan," Gabriel reassured.

I choked back my dread and searched the landscape for the birds.

"Down there." Atticus pointed. "We rose above them to catch them off guard."

I gulped. "This time, do I have to catch one and ummm..." I hesitated. I knew I would have to eat my catch eventually, but with the way my stomach flip-flopped, I would rather just be a vegetarian for the rest of my life. I'd never eaten anything I'd caught before. The idea of it seemed wrong, yet I knew the food at home had probably been alive before it became my meal.

"That's up to you, Deglan. If you're hungry, you'll know what to do. Otherwise, it's just an agility exercise. Your reflexes are tuning into your mind and if you can catch a bird mid-flight, I have no doubt you can defend yourself mid-attack from another dragon."

I gulped again. *Yeah, about that.* I knew what they expected me to do, but I still had a difficult time accepting it. *Surely, there are more qualified dragons who could overthrow Lord Edric.*

I searched below and spied a white albatross flapping just under the edge of the clouds. I took a deep breath and shifted my wings to catch the draft just above the bird, careful not to move my wings more than necessary to make him aware the hunting had begun. I flew steady for thirty seconds, deciding what the best plan should be. If I pounced on him from the top, grabbing him with my talons, I wouldn't have to see his beak or the look on his terrified face. However, I hadn't practiced flying with anything in my talons without destroying it.

I glanced at Atticus and Gabriel above me, watching my progress. I groaned and immediately wished I hadn't, because the bird turned sideways and our eyes met. The bird darted toward the ocean. I didn't hesitate, but took off, my wings raking powerfully at the air, pressing through the jet streams, and rocketing after the frightened bird.

I sped toward the powerful bird, pushing myself faster. I knew now why they wanted me to go after one of those. If I wouldn't have been so intent on catching the darn thing, I would have marveled at the albatross' speed. It tucked its wings down beside it and picked up speed, just a league or so from the ocean. I panicked. If he made it to the ocean he would go straight in. The albatross was an excellent diver, but I was not. The only time I'd been in the water was to bathe or skip rocks. I'd never held my breath or even tried to swim. I tucked my wings beside me as the bird had, the air rippling over my scales and down my body. I whipped my tail like a paddle in the warm air, which brought me within striking distance from the bird.

The salt from the ocean waves pummeled my face. I had to decide what to do if I didn't catch it. *Do I allow it to believe it won when it darts into the water. Or do I go after it? It's not far-fetched for a dragon to dive into the water; we are land, air, and water creatures by nature.*

The albatross turned its head, his eyes narrowed and... *did he just stick his tongue out at me?* I growled, and before I knew it, plunged into the surf after him. In the water, I had the advantage over the diving bird, the weight of my body moving me faster than his. He panicked and tried to shove his way to the top to escape, but I was too fast.

In one snap of my jaws the ornery bird was an afternoon snack, and boy did it taste good fresh.

I sprang from the water just as quickly as I'd entered, doing flips in the air as I flew toward the other dragons high above the clouds.

"Woo!" I exclaimed when I came into line with them. "That was amazing!"

"You did it, Deglan!" I could hear the pride in Atticus' voice.

"I can't believe you got it on your first try," Gabriel said, trying to hide his disbelief.

"It was amazing. One minute I was contemplating letting him go, the next I was picking his feathers from my teeth."

They laughed, happy my training had gone so well. I was happy with myself too.

My reverie broke when I heard the piercing scream of Meia in my mind.

DEGLAN! Help!

"Meia's in trouble!" I cried. I didn't wait for a response. I pushed myself as hard as I could, soaring through the air toward Meia. I could tell by the emotions she transferred to me that she was more afraid than she'd ever been. I had to get to her. She didn't say, but I knew exactly what had attacked her.

Chapter Twenty - Six
MEIA - THE HUMAN

I pressed my forehead against the tree and closed my eyes, hoping the nightmare would go away.

The animal that charged us the night we'd arrived was back and stalking me like prey. Mrs. Bensen and I had been practicing throwing my new dagger at targets near the stream's edge when she was called away. I dipped my toes into the water, thankful for the break. Training was hard work. I had just rolled my jeans up when he crept out of the bushes. My small dagger sat on the opposite bank, too far for me to grab.

"Why would they leave a puny human alone in the forests of Zamen?" he said, his red eyes glowing in the afternoon light. He circled me, licking his lips, probably imagining what I would taste like.

DEGLAN! Help! I screamed through my mind, hoping he was close enough for the link to work.

"Yes, call upon your dragon to help you, but I know for a fact he is far away and won't arrive in time to save you."

My heart crawled into my throat, and I knew he was right. I hadn't sensed Deglan's presence for hours. I swallowed hard, trying to remain calm. I knew Mrs. Bensen would be back soon. If I could distract him long enough she would help.

"What... do you... want?" The words came out in shaky intervals between my breaths.

"Lunch. A human lunch," he said and licked his lips again. "It's been too long."

"What are you?"

His maniacal laughter echoed in the small valley. "I'm something you should fear, the last of my kind. I've been hunting on Zamen Island for too long and the blood of the animals here runs cold. It's time for warmth." He stalked closer. The glint of the sun shone on his midnight-colored fur. He looked like an extremely large variety of dog with his long snout, similar to a wolf, but something about his tail and paws told me he wasn't any dog I'd ever seen. Judging by his body size, I debated quickly on my surroundings. The ancient trees had crevices, just large enough for my body and he wouldn't be able to follow.

I dashed from the water and ran between the clusters of trees. He lunged but crashed into the narrow opening with a thud. He snarled and his razor sharp claws tore the bark into bits. I raced forward and spied a large tree with a hole in the base. I scurried inside and pressed myself to the back of the hollow trunk.

He rammed against the tree and it crumpled under his bulk. The debris toppled in every direction, causing a monsoon of bark to shower upon us. A large branch crashed on his back, stunning him. I scrambled from the ruptured tree and pulled myself up another nearby. My mind struggled for a plan as my arms struggled with climbing. I pulled myself higher and higher, watching the creature shake the remaining rubble off his large body. He raced after me. His claws grabbed the aged bark, ripping it off as he climbed. He laughed, inching closer.

WHOOSH.

The sound echoed in the small valley and a blur of motion caused my pursuer to lose his hold. He tumbled through the branches and hit the ground with a thunderous boom. He staggered to his feet, shaking his large head and whimpering.

Something had hit him.

The trees were quiet, but the creature jumped in circles, head whipping in every direction, waiting for whatever it was to attack again.

WHOOSH.

Streaks of blue appeared, then disappeared into the

thick leaves. The creature darted for me again, this time with renewed strength and purpose. I screamed and scrambled higher as the creature climbed fast and hard. WHOOSH. The sound echoed again.

"DEGLAN! HELP!" I screamed, as the creature's claw swiped for my bare foot, missing it by only inches.

A thunderous roar ripped through the air as Deglan raged forward and clutched the creature's back, pulling him off the tree and to the ground. They crashed to the earth, then both twisted to their feet, poised to attack.

Deglan stalked the creature on all fours, a menacing growl pulsating through the air. Smoke billowed from his nostrils and his eyes flared red.

The creature looked like a small dog with its hackles raised, locked in a death stare with Deglan. He lunged with a hiss, but Deglan was ready and whacked him on the side with his tail. The beast flew into the trees, a whimper echoing in the small valley. It bolted from the brush and charged Deglan in full gallop, snarling as he launched. Deglan leaned down, led with his longest horns, and attacked. He jumped and Deglan pierced him in the stomach. The creature yelped in pain, stuck on Deglan's horns, flailing at Deglan's back with his claws.

Deglan roared in pain and flung him across the clearing into the tree I'd been hiding in. Tremors rippled up the limbs, shaking me loose from the branches. I grasped for a branch and sharp twigs cut into my palms. My feet dangled before my toes gripped another branch below me. I heard a series of cracks and felt the tree give way under my feet.

"Deglan!" I screamed.

The creature roared forward and hit Deglan in the chest, knocking him backward. Deglan hopped to his feet and growled. He drew to his full height, his eyes dancing with fire. His nostrils flared and smoke black as night emptied into the crisp air. His chest expanded and when he pushed the air out, a growl vibrated the air. Fire spewed from his lips and the creature jumped to the side before becoming a creature-kabob. Pinned against a tree, it cowered in fear. Deglan defeated him with one final blow. A small whimper escaped the creature before it lay lifeless under Deglan's paw.

"DEGLAN!" I screamed, as my hands slipped from the branch and I fell through the trees, plummeting toward the earth. In a mere second, he held me in his arms. His eyes returned to their familiar yellow as he looked down at me and smiled.

"You're safe now."

Chapter Twenty - Seven
DEGLAN - THE DRAGON

My heart raced as I set Meia on steady ground. Atticus landed behind us and shape shifted into his human form, then scooped up Meia, calming the hysterics that over took her small body. Gabriel landed moments later and assessed the injuries I'd sustained, but was pleasantly surprised when he found nothing more than a scratch. I'd been too fast for the creature, he hadn't stood a chance.

"If the albatross capture hadn't confirmed your hunt training was complete, this victory will," Gabriel said, patting my back. "Well done, Deglan. Well done."

News of the victory over the creature traveled through the island faster than wildfire. Seemed the creature, referred to as a werewolf, had been plaguing the island for many years and no one had been able to defeat it. The Zamens gathered in the streets, applauding and praising me for my bravery. Instead of being wary of the oversized dragon strolling in their midst, hope filled their eyes. Hatchlings shuffled in rank behind us, pretending to be an army at my command.

With every step towards Sterling's dwelling, with every cheer, with every nod of acceptance I received, courage built into the places I'd previously had none. Maybe I could do this. Maybe I could be lord of the unified clans. Though I still felt insignificant, I did feel stronger then I had days earlier.

As we walked, murmurs of the possible unification buzzed in the air. I pulled the excited voices to my ears and smiled when every one was welcoming of the new destiny set before them. Brick by brick, the wall of my courage grew.

At the gate, I turned and played the part of commander to dismiss the army. Hatchlings scattered in every direction, giggling or marching on their merry way.

We sat around the fire, talking about the days past and the ones yet to come. Meia was quiet and I could feel the tension in her body as she gripped the mug in her hands. She was upset at herself for her behavior in the clearing.

"You know, if I'd had my new dagger, I might've not been such a baby," Meia said, as if she knew I'd been eavesdropping on her thoughts.

"You know how to use a dagger?" I said, turning a curious eye on her.

"I didn't before today." She hopped from the log, a smile now plastered on her face. "You want to see what I've learned?" She didn't wait for a response before she set up targets on the opposite side of the courtyard.

I watched in amazement as Meia hit every mark while running, jumping, and even dodging pretend animals that lunged for her. Indeed, if she'd had her dagger, she would have been more of a challenge for the creature, and she knew it. She was proud to show her skills and accepted the praise graciously. When she turned at last towards me, my heart skipped a beat. She looked more like a warrior than the girl I'd met on Penrhyn and I too was very proud of who she'd become. Our eyes met and I didn't have to say a word. She knew.

\#

The next week passed in a blur with all the extra training and preparing for the coming lunar eclipse. A leathersmith fashioned a Meia-sized harness for my back. It would protect her from turbulent air currents or anything else that made my flying erratic.

Meia's aim with her dagger became more precise and I began to enjoy the albatross as an afternoon snack with little effort. I'd even caught a few rabbits. While not as tasty as the albatross, they were definitely a great hunt now that I knew what I was doing.

I stood at the mouth of a stream washing my claws and glimpsed my reflection. I really had changed. Would my parents even recognize me? What about Lord Edric? Would he even put up a fight seeing the sheer size of my body and jaws? I hoped not, but as Sterling said, we had to be prepared for a fight. The thought of attacking Lord Edric still churned my stomach, but they assured me that with my new skills, it would be an easy victory.

The day of the lunar eclipse arrived and we discussed our plans in Sterling's courtyard that afternoon, running over each exit route if Lord Edric reacted badly.

"We aren't going to attack," Atticus said, sharpening Meia's dagger. "We're going to reveal that the legend has come to pass and hope he recedes."

Lord Edric had been lord over the Teken for over three hundred years; I had a feeling he wasn't just going to give up his position for a tenth year. "He knew this day was coming. He's been eliminating dragons way before my time. I don't think he'll think twice about attacking." I thumped my claw on the log beside me. "What about the Lord of Zamen? Why doesn't he care that we're on his land training with plans to unify the clans?"

Gabriel grinned and cast a sideways glance at Atticus.

"What?" I looked at Meia, who also grinned like she knew something I didn't.

"Sterling is the Lord of Zamen," Mrs. Bensen said after a long pause. "And you know very well he welcomes the unification."

"What?" I could hardly believe it. Sterling seemed so... normal. He didn't act like a dragon lord and I hadn't heard anyone call him lord since I'd been on Zamen. "How can that be?"

"He's a humble lord, appointed well before our times. His Marvel skills came in handy throughout his reign, but he's ready for the change in power... and believes in you and the legend. He knows you will grow to be what the dragons need."

"Even though I'm ten," I said, disbelief mixing with my voice.

"Even though you're ten," Atticus said, sticking the dagger into its sheath. "Maybe even because you're ten. Your mind hasn't been corrupted by the ways of the world. You're pure and have something others don't."

"What's that?"

Atticus shrugged and grinned. "I'm sure you'll figure it out."

I groaned. That was everyone's answer for everything these days. You'll get it. You'll figure it out. You'll see. Why couldn't someone just stick up a sign with all the answers? It would be much easier that way.

"Deglan, you have another bit of magical training you need to do before we leave tonight."

My heart rate quickened at the way he said "magical training." If I weren't mistaken, I thought I saw him glance at Mrs. Bensen in human form when the words came out of his mouth. It would be the coolest thing to be able to shift. Then maybe Meia and I could really be friends. It was hard being twenty feet taller than my best friend. I paused, a smile crawling across my face. She was truly my best friend. We'd shared so much, even before we'd met, that it was hard to imagine my life without her.

"Hey, Deglan?" Meia's voice carried to my ears like a melodious tune.

She walked toward me, dressed not as I'd seen her before, in human garments, but in warriors clothing — blue britches and a black shirt with a leather belt that held her dagger. Her brown hair was pulled back into a tight bun and her sun-coated cheeks looked proud and ready for battle.

And battle we would... together.

Chapter Twenty - Eight
MEIA

Deglan stood in front of me admiring my new clothes, it made me feel ashamed that I'd agreed to wear them at all. I thought I looked foolish, as if I tried to be someone I wasn't. Mrs. Bensen assured me it was necessary. The chain mail fabric was soft as cotton, but no sword could penetrate it. Which meant no dragon or creature could either.

What I wouldn't have given for these clothes a week ago; maybe I wouldn't have acted like such a baby. I scolded myself, remembering the way I'd screamed and hid from the creature. I supposed it was natural, but I wasn't normal; I was part dragon. Definitely not a dragon reaction. *Had Deglan not arrived when he did...* I pushed the thoughts away and focused on my large, blue best friend standing in front of me.

"Can I talk to you for a minute?" I asked timidly, after realizing I'd just interrupted my father. It was still weird to think of this man as my flesh and blood, seeing him both as a pearl white dragon and a regular human man, but as the days passed, I began to see resemblances to myself in his actions. He often pointed out when I did something that reminded him of my mom. Her name was Arabella and he assured me I was just as beautiful as she had been.

"Sorry," I apologized.

"Nope, it's fine. We're done." He handed me my newly sharpened dagger and I placed it in my belt, then motioned for Deglan to follow.

We walked toward the familiar clearing the creature had attacked from, silent as we sat by the bank of the stream.

I hesitated, unsure how to start the conversation. My

father and Mr. Bensen thought it was necessary that I prepare him for the inevitable, but it was going to be hard. I'd already done my share of crying and pleading my case, but in the end, though it was painful to admit, I knew they were right.

"Deglan, do you realize I'm human?"

He laughed, "Umm, yup. I think I realize that."

I grinned. I wanted him to be smiling when I shared the news. I hesitated but knew if I didn't just blurt it out, I would lose my nerve.

"Deglan, after we are done on Teken Island... I've got to go back to California."

"What? Why?" The tone of his voice raised and worry crawled across his brow.

"Everyone says I have to grow up." I wanted to stomp my feet and protest the words coming out of my own mouth, but I knew I couldn't. As much as I wanted to stay in this adventure, I knew another waited for me at home. One called fifth grade. Ugh. "I mean, they're probably right. Ten might be just about full grown for a dragon, but it's not for us humans."

I watched his heart break and leak out of his almond-shaped eyes. I had to turn away. I couldn't let him see me cry; after all, we would still see each other as often as we wanted. I would have a dragon for a caregiver. I could just hop on Dad's back and come for a visit.

"Why can't you just stay on Teken Island? Your dad can stay too, and I can see you every day."

I twisted around and cocked my head to the side. "Sure, I'll be so happy being the only human on the island."

"We can get more!"

"You can't just order them up on the Internet or something. I need time to experience normal stuff before I become a dragon island adoptee. I need time to be me."

It broke my heart to speak it aloud, but it was pretty clear this was the way it had to be.

"I—" his voice broke and tears ran down his blue

cheeks.

I rushed to him. He took me in his big arms and held me to his chest. My head rested on him and I heard his heart beating in rapid thumps. I felt his pain coupled with the smallest bit of understanding flowing through his veins. He knew it would be all right eventually. We were best friends and nothing could change that.

"I know you have to go... but I don't have to like it. Maybe if I just give you some of my blood..." He let me down from his arms and gave me a sly grin.

"I have to be honest; the thought did cross my mind, but something inside me says I need to go back and experience what life has for me as a regular human before I try my feet out as a dragon." I bumped into his leg and smiled up at him. "Besides, we're linked. Even if I wanted to escape you, I couldn't. You're always in my head."

We sat beside the stream in silence, enjoying our last moments of quiet together.

The lunar eclipse had snuck up on me. Really, I needed a few more days before we headed out. But it was here... the morning before we had to leave and dethrone a dragon lord.

This was going to be one heck of a night.

DEGLAN

It was hard to push off Zamen Island and head home, knowing what waited for me there. The whole clan would be gathered at the Rising Ceremony, looking to Lord Edric for guidance. I had no assurance they would listen to me, but I had to try. Our whole race depended on it.

Meia crouched in the saddle on my back, and when her hands touched my scales, instead of fear or apprehension there was courage. She believed in me more than she ever had. We'd both dreamed last night and our mothers joined us. They walked us through both islands, showing us the land and its beauty. Then the dream shifted and showed us the difference in the oppression and fear on Teken under

Edric's lordship. My mother told me she was proud of who I'd become and would grow to be, reaffirming I had been chosen as the one to unify the clans. It should have relieved my fears, but it didn't. I still couldn't get over the fact that I was supposed to be the ruler of a whole species. The clear blue familiar waters of the Pacific Ocean below told me I needed to accept it quickly, because in less than an hour we would land on Teken Island.

MEIA

I felt the tension in every stroke of Deglan's wings as we flew toward his destiny. He was afraid; I couldn't say I blamed him. If someone told me I would have to rule over not only the whole fifth grade, but the entire school, maybe even every school next year, I think I would have a mental breakdown. I tried to have courage for him, knowing he could do anything, and I hoped it was working. At least if I was confident, he would feel it and it would rush through his veins like his fear rushed through mine now.

The dream had been amazing and frightening. Seeing my mom for the first time and feeling her embrace made me believe I could do anything. She told me how proud she was of what I'd become and was sorry she couldn't be there for me. She also told me that when I returned to Teken Island, the Dragon's Promise could no longer protect me.

I awoke in a cold sweat and crept from my bed to find Sterling, who'd known I would come. He was vague in his explanation, but confirmed the Promise would be lifted the moment I reached the island. I begged him to keep the information quiet. I knew the only reason I was allowed to go on the trek to Teken Island was because they believed my Dragon's Promise would protect me. But Sterling assured me he had no intention of ratting me out. He believed this path was as much my destiny as it had been Deglan's.

Deglan hadn't experienced this part of the dream, nor did I share it with him. He had enough to deal with then to worry about me. I would be okay as long as I was with Deglan. The confidence I felt, regardless of losing the Promise, ran through me like an I.V. of life, strengthening my resolve. Deglan felt it too. Surely, Lord Edric would not try to kill me again.

The chill of the night pressed in from all sides and the waters below us trembled with the pull of the rising eclipse. We were close now, and I felt it.

DEGLAN

My breath caught in my throat when Teken Island came into view. Meia placed her hands on my sides and calm rushed over me; she believed I could do it. By sheer size alone, I could probably defeat the dragons of the Teken Clan one by one, but if they all attacked at once, I doubt I'd have a chance. I really hoped it wouldn't come to that.

Sterling told me to approach it democratically. Explain the legend and ask for those who would stand behind me to speak out. If Lord Edric wouldn't step down, then we would use force to convince him.

"There's the island," I said loud enough for those in the front party to hear. "The Rising Ceremony takes place on the northernmost beaches."

"We'll fall back and let the others know," Gabriel said. "You and Meia land first. It will make Edric nervous about what reinforcements you brought. We'll watch carefully from the air until you signal us to land. The others will hang back until they're needed."

I took a deep breath and wagged my head. I glanced over my shoulder at the handful of Zamen dragons joining us that night, thankful they saw eye-to-eye with Lord Sterling and the legend. Matthew, Godfrey, and Jemes led the force, ready to help when needed.

"Deglan, we believe in you." Mrs. Bensen's voice carried through the wind to my ears.

With my head pointed down, Meia close to my back to break any resistance, I shifted my weight and sped toward the Rising Ceremony. The dragons gathered there looked up when we drew near. First, it was only a few, but as the murmur of the monstrous blue dragon rippled through the crowd, the music stopped and all eyes turned toward the sky. The only pair of eyes I dreaded glared at me — Lord Edric. I circled the ceremony once, then landed as gracefully as I could on the beach.

"Deglan, back for the Rising Ceremony?" Lord Edric said, moving across the beach with haste. "You'll have to get in line with the other hatchlings and wait your turn." He spat his words and pointed to the cowering line of tenth years.

I searched every face until I came to the one I'd been looking for. Carik stood last in the line, his eyes round with surprise. I could tell by his expression he was shocked to see my growth and I hoped he could tell by mine that I was relieved to see him alive. I pulled my gaze from Carik and back to Lord Edric.

Whispers rolled through the crowd when Meia hopped from my back and stood beside me, unafraid. She looked over the awestruck crowd then into the surprised face of Lord Edric. I knew I needed to say something, but it was everything I could do not to tremble.

A curious buzz of voices echoed through the crowd. My trembling stopped, and I pulled my body to full height.

MEIA

Landing on the beach next to two thousand dragons should have sent me screaming, but after everything I'd been through the past few weeks of my life, this was nothing. But hopping off Deglan's back knowing my Promise wouldn't protect me and still being bold, was the hardest thing I'd ever done.

When the dragon stalked forward and addressed Deglan, I knew exactly who he was, his pale green scales dull and lifeless in the moonlight. His eyes were a dry shade of yellow and his paws were wrinkled with time. He had to be at least a thousand years old.

I scanned the crowd and spied a dragon in the back that I recognized from the picture Deglan had found tucked in the pages of the diary. Deglan's mom watched, her eyes pinched together in the center. She looked fearful that her son was about to confront Lord Edric.

I could tell Deglan was afraid, so I knew I needed to speak up.

"Lord Edric?"

"Yes? And you are?" His eyes flitted to the back of my neck and I held my breath. Could he tell the Dragon's Promise was no longer valid? The way his eyes flickered, I couldn't be sure. However, I could tell he knew exactly who I was.

"Meia," I spoke through pursed lips. "The girl you tried to kill ten years ago."

Shockwaves of disbelief echoed through the clan.

"It's true!" Deglan's father called over the crowd, silencing the protests.

"You have no proof!" Edric shot back, pointing his claw.

A curious buzz of voices echoed through the crowd. Deglan pulled himself to full height and looked straight at Lord Edric, who snarled.

"I do have proof," Deglan said, motioning at the sky.

On cue, my father and the Bensens landed on the beach behind Deglan and the other Zamens now circled the ceremony.

Gasps of horror came from every direction when they looked up and saw the dragons above.

"I am proof," my father said, transferring quickly into a human.

Lord Edric gasped and threw the scepter from his hand to the ground. "You should have both died!" he spat.

"They didn't, and now I'm here to relieve you of your throne," Deglan said, his voice wavering.

I reached over quickly and laid my hand upon Deglan's arm, willing all the courage I had to transfer into his body. At once, his face changed and determination narrowed his brows. He knew exactly what he was doing.

"Legend spoke of this day. A dragon has been born with links to the trinity clans — the Zamens, the Tekens, and the humans. We have come in peace, as long as peace is kept."

Lord Edric tightened his mouth and formed a thin line with his lips, but the crowd watched in admiration as Deglan continued.

"We all know what the legend claims and I'm here to announce it's here this night. The unification of the clans has arrived. Let us be rivals no more."

It took a moment for the realization to sink in, but when it did, the crowd roared in applause, startling Lord Edric. His face went from anger to betrayal in a matter of seconds.

"Stop this foolishness!" Lord Edric screamed, holding his hands up to quiet the excited crowd. "You have no authority to dethrone anyone, *hatchling*."

"But he does..." My father stepped up and stood next to Deglan.

"And who are you?" Edric spit.

"Once human, now I'm Zamen... and Meia's father."

The understanding raced across Lord Edric's face and a low guttural growl came from his jaws. He bared his teeth and his nostrils flared, sending rivulets of smoke trailing to the sky.

I stumbled backwards, frightened at the rapid change of Edric's eyes; it had come to force.

DEGLAN

Atticus moved forward and stood between the angry Lord Edric and myself.

"Edric, the day you took my wife's life and tried to take mine, you set into motion the legend that *is* coming to pass today, for I'm both Zamen and human, and she's my flesh and blood," he said, motioning for Meia.

"And I, Edric, am human and part Teken," Meia said,

standing next to her father. I could feel her fear as she stood there, but didn't understand it. *Why would she be afraid? Edric can't hurt her. Or can he?*

I pushed the uneasy feeling down and stood boldly behind Meia and her father, "And I, Edric, am Teken, Zamen, and part human." I turned toward the crowd, knowing what needed to happen now. "Teken clansmen, Edric knew this day was coming. He knows the legend well and has been eliminating Teken dragons from our land for many years. This Rising Ceremony has been a way for him to check the marks of your beloved hatchlings, then do away with them if they posed a threat." I looked at Edric, whose eyes gleamed red. "He tried to kill me the night I fled because he discovered I bore the ancient dragon mark."

The crowd silenced when I raised my arm to the sky. Some bowed at the sight of the legendary dragon on my forearm, while others just stared.

"Edric, by the legends claim, I hereby relieve you of your position."

No sooner had the words left my mouth before Edric lunged forward and grabbed Meia. The crowd recoiled in shock.

"I may not be able to kill her on my own, but I can torture her so she wishes I could." He growled and jumped from the ground.

Meia screamed and I took off after him, followed by every dragon that stood behind me.

MEIA

I'd barely realized what had happened before I felt his talons seize me. I screamed and tried to release the dagger in my belt, but his grip was so tight on my midsection that I couldn't loosen it. I flailed my arms and hit him trying to free myself.

"No!" I protested, tears erupting from my eyes as we rose high into the night sky. "Please! No!"

Edric didn't listen. His pale green body obscured the

rising lunar eclipse as he flew toward a destination unknown.

I heard a symphony of wings behind us, but couldn't see past his body to confirm who followed. He flew higher, the air got thinner and colder by the moment. I knew enough about earth science to know that if he went too far I wouldn't be able to breathe. Would this be the way he would kill me?

I struggled against his power, pushing, tugging, pulling, and scratching at his calloused scales. "Please!"

"You don't deserve to live," he snarled.

He flew higher and higher, the air thinned, and I began to choke from the lack of oxygen.

Edric laughed and continued rising.

My head swam and bright lights flashed before my eyes before everything went black.

DEGLAN

"What can we do, Deglan?" I heard as we flew at hasty speeds toward Edric, who clutched Meia in his talons. I looked behind me and saw the mass of dragons that followed, Tekens joined the Zamens, all in protection of Meia. The Tekens wanted the unification as much as the Zamens had.

"Some of you stay low and watch the skies. If he drops her, she can't hit the water or ground; she'll surely die. Some of you need to turn back and help the others in case Edric's follower's revolt."

"Some stayed behind and detained them," said a familiar voice nearest to me. It was my father.

"Branch out and try to corner him. We can't let him get away!"

"Deglan?" My dad's voice beckoned my attention. "The Dragon's Promise is gone," he said, sorrow filling his eyes. "It dissolved upon her arrival back on the island."

"What?!" The horror of the situation coursed fear through my veins. "How can that be?"

"It doesn't matter, get to her and save her!"

I pushed myself away from the pack, using my speed to gain on Edric. He rose into the atmosphere, and I immediately knew his intentions. He planned to suffocate her, a loophole in the Dragon's Promise he thought she still had protecting her life. I cried out in rage and pressed forward. I could see it was already working; Meia's body lay limp in his grasp.

The anger in me boiled and tremors rippled through my body. A new burst of strength shot through my veins, and I rocketed toward Edric, who hadn't realized I'd caught up so fast. I leeched onto his back with my talons. He shrieked and opened his claws. Meia's lifeless body plummeted toward the earth below.

"Catch her!" I screamed, forgetting about Edric in my grasp.

He whirled around and thumped me hard with his tail. I lost my grip and reeled backward. I rushed at him, screeching my fury, my jaws snapping for him. We locked arms and I slammed my tail into every part of his exposed body.

I had a size advantage over Edric, and I pummeled him over and over, pushing away his snapping jaws. I debated using fire, but the recoil would hit me too. A snarl grew in the depths of my belly. I pulled my lips over my teeth and pushed out the intense sound. My anger echoed in the thin air and my tail landed hard across his body. He squealed in pain and arched his back, and I lost my grip. He fell toward the earth flailing, trying to spread his torn wings. He plunged toward the earth, disappearing through the clouds. The battle had been won.

Applause erupted as soon as I came within view of Teken Island. I landed with a heavy thump and searched the crowd for Meia. I pressed through the dragons gathered in the clearing until she came into view. There on the sand under the rising lunar eclipse lay Meia, unconscious, but alive, and in the arms of my mother.

MEIA

Something wet rested on my forehead when I regained consciousness. The last thing I'd remembered was being in the clutches of... I sprang to my feet and instantly regretted it when the room spun like a dance. My head pounded and I struggled to remain upright.

"Meia! Lie back down," scolded Mrs. Bensen.

Relief washed over me like a tidal wave when I sat on the bed. I don't know how it happened, but I'd been rescued from Edric's clutches. "Is Deglan okay?" I said, still unwilling to open my eyes.

"Yes, he's fine. He's with... he's with your father. They are... well, I'll let them tell you the news."

"News? What news?" I pried open an eye, peeking at her.

Mrs. Bensen rubbed her hands together nervously. "They wanted to be the ones to tell you; I promised I wouldn't say anything," she said, biting her lip. "I was always terrible at keeping secrets." Her eyes darted for the window and she sighed. "They're here; I'll fetch Atticus."

My father came in the small room and sat on my bed. "Hey, how are you feeling?"

The pounding headache wanted me to tell him the truth, but I wasn't about to admit anything I didn't have to. "I'm okay. What's the news?"

He laced his fingers in mine and gave me a warm but weary smile. "Meia, I'm a dragon now."

"Yeah, I know," I said, interrupting him. "I've known that for a while now; this isn't news."

"Meia, I'm still learning how to control the transformation between human and dragon, and although the alliance between the dragons and humans now exists, it doesn't mean dragons are welcome living among them when they can't control when they will shed their human particles."

My heart pounded in my chest at the revelation. "That means we get to stay with the dragons?" The happiness bubbled through my words.

"No," he said and looked at our hands. "You still need to go back to California with the Bensens until I can control this. It wouldn't be safe for me there, and you need to go back and grow up before becoming tied to the dragon life."

"But I'm already tied," I protested, tears springing to my eyes. "I've got dragon in me. Lord Sterling said it, and you know it—"

"But you aren't a dragon."

I grabbed at my father and held him. "I don't want to lose you again. Not when I've just found you."

"You won't lose me again. Not ever. The Bensens will bring you back whenever you want."

"But they can't without the social worker's approval and..." The words came out laced with hysteria. "I know my social worker; she would never let me leave the country *that* often."

"Meia," he said, grasping my shoulders to look me in the face. "I have asked them to adopt you."

"What? Why? You're alive!" I struggled to understand why we were having this conversation.

"Because if they're your legal parents, they can bring you anywhere they want, anytime they want, and they won't have to answer to a grumpy social worker."

Tears flooded my eyes. "But I just want to be with you."

"I know," he said, running his hands through my hair, "and I promise you, there will be a time when we'll be together again here with the dragons. Together for good. But for now, I need you to trust me and go back home with the Bensens. Let them adopt you. I need you to do this for me and trust that we'll be together again."

"When?" I sat back and spit the word out like a spoiled child.

My father laughed jubilantly and pulled me close again. "I'm not sure, but a Dragon's Promise stands." He pulled my head to him and placed a kiss on the back of my neck.

A tingle shot down my spine and I knew a new Promise of protection had been placed upon my life.

Chapter Twenty - Nine
DEGLAN - THE DRAGON

The afternoon breeze blew through the island and with it the hope of a new life and unified clan. I'd already seen the changes in just twenty-four hours. Dragons were happier.

Carik shared with me how he'd escaped detection that fateful night. He'd watched the confrontation from the base of the cliff, hiding in the nearby trees. Lord Edric led the clan to believe I'd died, but he'd seen me fall and knew I'd flown away. He'd gone to my parents right away, assuring them I'd gotten away safely. He apologized for whatever role he played in that night, but I assured him that in the end, it was how it was supposed to be.

I saw Jemes with his wife and hatchlings. Watching them laugh and play made everything that had happened in the past month all worth it.

"Deglan?" Meia's voice broke my reverie.

"Meia!" I called for her.

Meia ran toward me and I scooped her up in my arms and laughed.

"You're okay!" she said, hugging me tight.

"As are you!" I said and set her back on the ground. She was my best friend, probably the best I'd ever had in my whole life.

"Did you hear my news?" She asked, a sour look scrunching her face.

"Yes and I think it's a good idea. At least for now." I said, wondering if Atticus had told her everything.

"How can you say that! I think it's a terrible idea," she said and crossed her arms.

I cocked my head and pinched one eye shut. I could tell

by her body language that she'd already accepted the news.

"I don't want to talk about it. Nothing I can say will make them change their minds." She flopped onto the nearby stump in a huff. "Hopefully your news is better than mine. Anything would be better than this."

"I guess it could be better," I said, unsure if it truly was. "Meia, I... I appointed your father lord of the unified clans."

"What?" The disbelief in her voice ruptured the air. "Why?"

"I don't know. I mean, I know your dad is wise and will rule fairly, but it just felt right. I might be the one from the legends, and I might be ready to rule a whole clan of dragons, but... I had this feeling that it wasn't quite my time yet. Like I needed to have another couple of adventures, or something. I don't know." I watched her face for understanding.

"Wow. My dad is Lord of the Teken?" A proud smile lit up her face.

"Well, actually, at the council meeting this morning they changed their name. No longer are they Zamens or Tekens. Each island will retain its name, but they're going to become a new unified clan under a new name." The heat rose to my cheeks. I hoped and prayed she wouldn't ask what the name was. It was embarrassing enough already.

"What did they choose?" She tilted her head sideways and grinned in my direction. I had a feeling she already knew.

"We're now called... The Clan of Deglan." I rolled my eyes.

"Ooh! What a perfect name, Deglan!" She hopped to her feet and hugged my torso. "Perfect! Perfect! Perfect!" She clapped her hands and jumped in unison.

"I'm not so sure about perfect. I was outvoted."

"No, it's sooo perfect. It was because of your Rising that they unified... Deglan, it's perfect!"

I frowned. "Well, I have no say in it now; it stuck. They

are already changing signs. Sterling was also part of the council who approve it."

There was an awkward silence between us as we both contemplated how our lives had changed in a little under a month.

"Deglan, I've got to go soon. We have to file the adoption paperwork before school starts in the fall, and I guess we have to be there to do it. I've got to get used to being human again," she said sadly.

"I know, Meia. But Lord Atticus says I can go see you anytime I want and that you'll be able to come here soon anytime you want." Saying it made it real and a wave of sadness washed over me. Meia was leaving the island.

"Will our link work from here to California?" she asked, kicking the rock in front of her.

"It should, which means we can still talk to each other."

She let out a long, labored sigh. "I guess there is only one way to find out."

"If it doesn't work, they can't keep us apart that long. You're my best friend. I'll make them bring you back. You're part dragon after all, you belong here."

"Promise?"

"Promise. You and I are dragons forever."

We both looked at each other for a moment, then I scooped her up and held her tight.

Chapter Thirty
MEIA - THE HUMAN

"I can't believe summer's over," Cate groaned, shuffling her feet on the sidewalk in front of school. "At least you got to travel the South Pacific. I didn't get to do anything quite that exciting... unless playing the violin badly to annoy my brother counts."

I giggled. If only she knew just how exciting my summer had truly been. "As I said before, it was pretty cool, but the humidity definitely takes some getting used to."

"Did you get to go snorkeling?"

"I tried, but I couldn't do it. Instead, I collected shells and made some friends."

I laughed again. Mrs. Bensen had told me to keep my dragon news quiet. Besides, if I told Cate I'd found out I was part dragon, she would flip out and think I was insane. Though, knowing Cate, she would probably just let it roll off her back like another crazy thing Meia believes.

Mrs. Keller was cheery when we passed her in the hall. "Meia. Cate. How was your summer?" she asked.

"Boring," Cate said, sounding like she wanted to puke.

I looked past her to see a brown-haired boy, about my age, talking with the principal, Mr. Banks. He looked up, his bright blue eyes twinkling when he caught my glance. I quickly looked back to Cate and Ms. Keller.

"Meia, what about you?"

"Oh. Uhh, my foster parents decided to adopt me," I said, sensing the boy was looking at me again.

"What?! Meia you didn't tell me that," Cate said, grabbing at my arm and jumping up and down. "Why didn't you tell me? That's huge news!"

"Meia, that's great! Congratulations," Mrs. Keller said

and patted my arm warmly. "Mr. and Mrs. Bensen are wonderful people."

"Yeah, they're pretty cool. They took me to the Cook Islands this summer. It was what you would call... a real bonding experience." *I mean, after all, I found out they were dragons, I found my dad, I found out I was part dragon, we fought together... definitely bonded.*

The bell rang, announcing our need to get to our homeroom. Fifth grade had officially begun.

Cate and I shared homeroom teachers again and found the seats with our names taped to the surfaces of the desks. Luckily, the teacher put them in alphabetical order and we were only one seat apart. Meia Bensen and Cate Cartwell.

The seat in the middle of us had a label, but it was covered by a student enrollment packet.

"Fabulous, we have a new student sitting between us," I whispered loud enough for Cate to hear. "I hope she's nice and will pass notes."

"Not like that snotty Patricia Tison," Cate whispered, thumbing at the snob of the fifth grade.

I turned toward Patricia, who was flipping her hair and talking with Kevin Wallace, the boy behind her. When Kevin rolled his eyes and shook his head, Cate and I laughed.

"Too bad he got stuck sitting next to her," I said and giggled again.

Our fifth grade teacher shuffled into the room and wrote *Mrs. Gardner* in big bubbly letters on the board. She looked around the classroom, at all the faces in the chairs. The only vacant seat was the new kid's.

"Good morning, fifth graders."

"Good morning, Mrs. Gardner," we all said in unison.

"It's going to be another couple of minutes before we will start. The new student is getting some help with his locker."

His locker?

I groaned and looked at Cate.

A boy. We were going to be separated by a boy. Fifth grade was already promising to be absolutely miserable. I didn't know any boy that would pass notes for a girl. Most of them just tattle or read the notes to their friends.

I slouched in my seat and leaned on my wrist, looking at Cate. I rolled my eyes and made my typical 'he's got cooties' face to see if she would laugh.

The door to the classroom creaked and I popped up to see the dark-haired boy I'd spied with the principal earlier, step through the large brown door. He looked around the room and stopped when his eyes met mine.

He looked familiar, yet I knew I'd never seen this boy before.

Mrs. Gardner went to the door and led him forward.

He looked as if he was going to puke from anxiety, but his eyes never left mine.

"Class, we have a new student in the school this year. I would like you all to make him feel welcome. He just moved into the neighborhood and is probably a little intimidated by all the new faces. Would you like to introduce yourself?" she asked the nervous boy.

The buzz around the classroom was loud, but the boy still hadn't released my eyes from his locked stare.

"I... I guess," he said, clutching the backpack in his arms that matched his blue eyes. "Hi, everyone." A wide smile broke across his lips, but he never looked away. "I'm Deglan." His eyebrows wagged in my direction when the shock registered on my face.

No. Way.

TO BE CONTINUED...

Artist Index

Made in the USA
Lexington, KY
14 December 2011